Controlled Desire

FALL OF DESIRE SERIES

DARIE MCCOY

Edited by: All That's Wright

Cover Art/Design: A.S. McCoy

ISBN

Paperback: 978-1-961999-03-9

Ebook: 978-1-961999-08-4

Welcome to Club Desire

"Welcome to the world of Club Desire, one of the world's most exclusive BDSM clubs. We cater to your pleasure and your pain. We have everything you could possibly desire."

CLUB DESIRE

*It's never too late to explore your true desires. **Live!***

Note from the author

Please note this is a work of fiction. It should not be used as a how-to guide for participating in the BDSM lifestyle. As with all things, it is recommended for anyone wishing to participate in similar activities to do their own research on the subject. Again, this isn't a guide. It is for entertainment purposes only.

Prologue

Maria Elena Stokes looked at the package her friend sent her with skepticism. Tahlia was determined to, as she said, put some umph back into Maria's life. As far as Maria was concerned, her life had plenty of umph. *Didn't it?*

Well aware that her friend's idea involved spicing up her love life, Maria hesitated to even open the envelope. It had been almost three years since her husband Oscar was taken from them in a tragic car accident. Maria would trade the insurance and settlement money to have her sweet partner back. But, that wasn't how life worked.

Instead, she'd gone on hiatus as the CEO of Fortitude Banking and focused on getting her son through his last year of high school. Jared was now in his sophomore year in college. He no longer needed her as much. Although he was less than an hour away, he lived in his own apartment off campus, so she didn't see him very often. She'd been back at the helm of the company for two years, guiding them through new acquisitions and expansions.

With the terms of the trust left by his father and the college fund they'd started for him when he was born, Jared didn't call her for money like most college students. He didn't spend his monthly stipend extravagantly. She tried to give him the privacy of not checking the balances of his accounts and trusting him to do what he was taught when managing his finances.

Fingering the package, Maria bit the bullet and broke the seal. Inside were papers folded together. Her fingers hovered over her phone with the urge to call Tahlia and demand she explain.

However, she knew her friend would simply ask if she read the document first. When Maria responded in the negative, Tahlia would just end the call. She didn't believe in answering questions if a person had the answer in front of them, but refused to look. It was funny when Tahlia did it to other people, but Maria didn't like being on the receiving end of that candor.

Maria scanned the first page, which was a letter from her friend. Her lips pursed as she wondered why Tahlia sent a physical letter instead of email or, better yet, calling her.

M.E.,

I know you have questions, the first probably being why did I write a letter instead of just talking to you. Well, I have been talking to you and you haven't been listening. So, I'm taking matters into my own hands. Included in the package with this letter is a questionnaire that you will fill out in its entirety. Don't have me make a special trip to make your ass comply. It is time for you to start living again. Not just being a mom and running a company. Really living. If the tables were reversed, and it had been you in that car instead of Oscar, you know damn well he'd already have a new wife. I don't mean to be harsh, but you know I'm right. (You also know I don't give a shit about fighting dirty.)

I'm not saying you need to go so far as getting a husband, heaven forbid. But you need to do something other than your B.O.B. So, I've purchased you a membership in an exclusive club. One where you can let your freak flag fly without judg-

ment. They have air tight NDAs that everyone has to sign to even get past the receptionist. It's invitation only. No regular degular tackhead is going to be in there.

To help you out, I've already lined up your first 'date.' He comes highly recommended for what I think you need. BE HONEST when you answer the questions on the questionnaire. There's even an option to do it electronically, but I know you. You like to have stuff in your hands so you can agonize over it for eighty years before you commit. Unfortunately, you don't have eighty years. You have two weeks. If you haven't responded by then, I'm coming to Logan City to get your ass in gear. Do NOT call me until you've read every single line on that questionnaire.

Love you to pieces! Mean it!

Tahlia

Maria dropped Tahlia's letter and the rest of the paper like they were burning her fingertips. Her heart started racing, and sweat popped out on her brow. The only two people she'd ever told about her fantasies were Tahlia and her late husband. Oscar had been a wonderful lover, but he hadn't been the most adventurous when it came to the bedroom. She always orgasmed, but he'd never pushed boundaries or made her want to stalk him to get another taste of the magic in his pants. Compared to some of the things she'd heard from other married women, she had an excellent set up. At least her husband knew how to make her come.

Was she brave enough to shed her inhibitions? Tahlia had done part of the work for her. All Maria had to do was take the leap. Willing the shaking of her fingers to stop, Maria picked up the first page of the questionnaire.

Chapter One

Maria sat in the backseat of the limo that picked her up from her hotel. Her fingers twisted together in her lap as she considered asking the driver to take her back. Stomach flipping nervously, she contemplated how long Tahlia would be mad at her if she chickened out. Then, she thought of how disappointed she'd be in herself for not being brave enough to take a chance on fulfilling a fantasy she'd had for many years.

Due to her job managing a banking conglomerate, she led people daily. Fortitude was on the cusp of profiting a billion dollars annually. Maria issued orders and stayed on top of trends to steer the Fortitude ship. To do those things, she had to remain in control every second. It was mentally exhausting, and she had very few contemporaries she trusted to vent to about her fatigue.

Squaring her shoulders, she took a deep breath as the vehicle rolled to a stop. When the door opened, she accepted the driver's assistance stepping out. The crisp Chicago wind caused the bottom of her calf length coat to whip against her bare legs. Tugging the sections closed again, she thanked him. It was pre-arranged for him to return when she texted.

Looking up at the three-story, red brick, building before her, Maria marveled at how normal it looked on the exterior. According to Tahlia, anything a consenting deviant little heart desired could be found here. As she approached the glass paned door, she noticed a black square plate affixed to the right of it. No words appeared on the plate. There was simply an intricate gold mask, just as Tahlia described.

Still giving herself an internal pep talk, Maria opened the door and stepped inside. The entrance gave no indication as to what type of business was beyond the reception area. Behind the desk was a pretty woman with blonde hair. When she noticed Maria, she smiled sweetly.

"Hello, Welcome to Club Desire, Mrs. Stokes. I'm Bethany. I've been expecting you."

Maria walked past the low tufted chairs to the near chest-high reception desk. Initially startled by the young woman appearing to know her name, she reminded herself of what Tahlia told her about her membership in the club. A photo was included in the information her friend provided them with when she purchased the membership. So, of course, Bethany would know who she was on sight.

"Please. Call me Maria."

Bethany nodded, then tapped away on the keyboard and clicked the mouse for a few moments before looking up again.

"Okay, Maria, I see you were gifted a membership by one of our long-time members Tahlia Lenore."

Bethany's smile hinted that Maria was more than lucky to have such a friend. She reached for a clipboard containing a stack of documents along with a pen.

"As part of our on-boarding process, you'll need to fill out some paperwork and sign the Non-Disclosure Agreement before we go any further. You can have a seat right over there to get started."

"Thank you." Maria accepted the clipboard with nary a tremble in her digits. She was proud the nerves of steel she used in her professional life made an appearance to help her make it through at least this part of the process.

After sitting in one of the offered chairs, Maria went through the pages of the intake paperwork reading each line carefully. She was oddly comforted by the attention to detail given to maintaining the privacy of anyone who entered Club Desire. A woman in her position had to be careful—especially with her company headquarters being located in the bible-thumping south.

Flying her freak flag had to be done with the strictest of discretion. Maria knew she wouldn't be given the slack of her white male counterparts if there was even a whiff of impropriety. Not that exploring her sexual desires as a single, consenting adult was anyone's business.

Once she was done with the documents, Bethany completed the process by reiterating the rules of the club—which Maria noted was verbatim to the information on the paperwork. She figured it was because far too many people wouldn't actually read everything before signing.

"I'll remind you, we are a private club, and all members and guests must adhere to all rules of this establishment. Is that understood?"

Maria nodded in response. There was nothing else to be said as she'd already agreed in writing. Bethany volunteered to show her around, but Maria declined. The 'date' Tahlia arranged for her was supposed to meet her in the first-floor lounge and do the honors.

"Okay, if you're sure." Bethany stretched one slender arm toward the hallway on the right.

A buzzer sounded allowing her entry past the black door at the end of the hallway. The same golden mask was displayed on the door. When Maria crossed the threshold, she immediately heard a sensual thumping baseline. The music wasn't dance-club loud, but it sent a pulsing feeling across her skin, and down her spine coalescing at her center.

Her eyes didn't know where to land as she studied the opulent interior of the lounge. The red sofas and chairs screamed 'sex'. According to the rules, no sex happened here, but the atmosphere was definitely set to get a person prepared for whatever might come. Waiters and waitresses moved around the room occasionally stopping to serve a drink or accept an order from a patron.

Maria couldn't stop herself from staring at the sculpted bare chests of the waiters. They could all be models with their cut physiques. The waitresses were stunning as well. They wore only black lace panties and bras with red bottomed heels. Knowing how much those shoes cost on the low end, let Maria know Club Desire didn't short change their staff.

People were scattered around the space. Some on the sofas in conversation, while others were seated in chairs or at the bar. The person she was set to meet stated she should have a seat at the bar and he would come to her.

Unable to suppress the compulsion to gawk at the statues behind the bar, Maria took a seat. She was thankful for the sturdy back on the stool since she wasn't sure she could keep the sides of her coat together while focusing on not falling off the seat.

She'd just gotten herself properly balanced when the bartender came over to her. The tattoos covering his muscular arms were eye-catching. Almost as much as his face and the rest of his body. It took supreme focus to understand the words tumbling from his lips.

"What can I get you, beautiful?"

Maria would've loved a shot of liquid courage. However, she ordered a ginger ale with a splash of grenadine instead. In her peripheral vision, she noticed a figure sliding onto the empty stool a couple of seats away from her. When the bartender placed her beverage in front of her, she used his retreat as an opportunity to peruse the stranger.

Although he wore a black suit, the purple pocket square, her date specified, wasn't present. Nor did he have tattoos along the backs of the long fingers laying on the bar top. Her gaze traveled upwards from the digits to the broad shoulders filling out the suit jacket to the square jawline accentuating kissable full lips. When his head rotated in her direction her breath caught in her throat while her heart started a thunderous rhythm in her chest.

In all of Maria's fifty-four years on earth, she'd never been so instantly drawn to anyone. A twinge of disloyalty pinged the back of her mind when she realized the feeling applied to her late husband as well. As crazy in love as she was with Oscar, he hadn't stolen her ability to breathe by existing in her space.

When the corner of the man's lips tipped up in advance of forming a panty-wetting smile, Maria snapped her eyes to the bubbles of the drink in her hands. Although there were hints of silver in the nearly black strands of his hair, he was obviously more than a few years her junior. Black don't crack and Asian don't raisin, but Maria didn't think it was genetics keeping his face so youthful looking. It was actual youth.

She didn't return his smile and her face heated with embarrassment at being caught staring. Maybe she wasn't cut out for being a member of a place like Club Desire. If a man smiling at her gave her the vapors would she actually be able to participate in any of the things her mind dreamed up while she was alone?

Maria's introspection was interrupted by warmth wrapping around the back of her neck. Her fingers flew to the area making contact with unknown digits.

"What the fuck?" The words flew from her mouth as she looked over her shoulder.

When she turned, she was nose to nose with a man wearing a harsh expression. She guessed he could be considered handsome, but that flew out of the window when he touched her without warning or permission.

Chapter Two

Ji-Yeong settled on going to the bar to have a drink and scope out the room before deciding if he wanted to go to one of the upper floors. Normally, he would have his scene already worked out and set up with a willing partner before he set foot into the lounge. He typically rotated companions to keep from giving anyone the impression he sought exclusivity.

Tonight, he hadn't made prior arrangements, because it was time to move on from his most recent playmate. She'd begun trying to coordinate their encounters with too much frequency. Unlike many men, Ji-Yeong wasn't ruled by his libido. He thoroughly enjoyed sex. More specifically, he enjoyed catering to a woman's pleasure during sexual experiences. But, if he didn't dip his pen in the ink every other day, he knew his dick wouldn't fall off from lack of use.

As he approached the bar, his gaze was drawn to a curvy form perched precariously on one of the high-backed seats. Her heeled feet were propped on the low railing running the length of the bar. The curve of her calf made his mouth water to lick the dip behind her knee to see if it was as sensitive as he imagined.

He sat a couple of seats away from her. He didn't even try to stop himself from visually appreciating the unknown beauty. Her face was new to him. But, it didn't necessarily mean she was new to Club Desire. There were some members who were comfortable dropping $250k on a membership to only partake one or two times a year. The lovely lady could be part of that contingent.

Ji-Yeong made his perusal beneath lowered lids with his head slightly turned away, but when he detected her looking at him, he lifted his eyes to meet hers. Her full lips made him imagine how they'd look when her face twisted in ecstasy. A distant second was the way they would stretch to accommodate his cock as she took his length between them.

Thinking of her mouth on him had the half grin he wore becoming a full-blown smile. The way she whipped her hazel eyes away from him answered his first question about her. She was definitely new to the club. Although her medium brown skin held a youthful glow, her carriage told him she was a minimum of forty years old. Where she landed was a mystery he'd have to solve later. It didn't matter. As long as they were consenting adults, he didn't have an upper limit on his partner's age. Younger...He didn't engage with anyone less than thirty.

While she concentrated on the beverage between her delicate fingers, Ji-Yeong considered the best way to engage. He wondered who'd sent her to a known BDSM club without an escort or some sort of security blanket to ease her into her first encounter.

In his opinion, that wasn't how things were done. He'd never send an inexperienced Sub into an unfamiliar environment. They were already in their heads trying to decide if they really wanted to take the leap. The last thing a Dom, who cared about their Sub, should do is heighten their fear and uncertainty. Unless it was what the Sub requested. Somehow, Ji-Yeong didn't think his Beauty had made such a request.

A frown put a crease between his eyebrows when a man approached the bar and grabbed Beauty by the back of her neck. Ji-Yeong barely heard her exclamation of "What the fuck?" before he was out of his seat snatching the man away from her.

The guy stumbled back a couple of steps, then squared his shoulders, standing straight and glaring at Ji-Yeong.

"What the fuck is wrong with you dude? Why are you putting your hands on me?"

Ji-Yeong assumed the same posture, putting himself between Beauty and the jackass.

"You have issues with me putting hands on you, but you walked up to this woman and touched her inappropriately? Make that make sense." The growl in Ji-Yeong's voice made it clear it wasn't a friendly request.

The two were drawing attention. Ji-Yeong didn't want trouble in the club, but the asshole didn't look even a little contrite about breaking the rules. Ji-Yeong would definitely have a talk with Elijah about this. The owner of Club Desire didn't tolerate the defiance of club rules. They were there for everyone's protection.

"Chill out, man. She's my date. She wants me to be a little rough. She likes it."

"Usually, when someone wants something, they don't respond with 'What the fuck' when it happens."

Turning slightly so that he could see both the jackass and Beauty, he stared into her face with a single lifted eyebrow. She met his gaze before her eyes shifted to the jackass.

"I never said I wanted someone to grab me by my neck unawares. I don't even know you." While the volume of her voice was low, the edge of her words was sharp. She wasn't playing a role.

"What? It's me. Sinister. I'm the Dom you came here to meet." In obvious frustration, he gestured to his clothing.

"I'm wearing the damn suit, with the fucking pocket square." Wiggling his fingers, palms facing him, he continued.

"Tattoos on the fingers. Ring a bell?"

Ji-Yeong had never heard of the guy, but he said his name as if everyone should know him. Ji-Yeong watched recognition filter into Beauty's expression only to be replaced by a sour expression. Jackass Sinister had arrogance pouring off of him. It was apparent to Ji-Yeong the guy fancied himself a real Dom. It was also clear that he considered his status elevated his above hers. The snide pitch of his voice was evidence enough.

"Miss, do you consent to continuing your association with this person?" Ji-Yeong addressed Beauty without turning his back completely on the jackass.

"Of course, she does. It was all arranged. I'm just giving her what she wants. Right, Marie?"

Ji-Yeong shot him a glare. "I didn't ask you. Unless you identify as a Miss, I was speaking to *her*." Ji-Yeong tilted his head toward Beauty.

When the guy went to speak again, Ji-Yeong put a hand directly in front of his face. Returning to Beauty, he lifted a single brow—waiting for her response.

"No. This isn't going to work. I didn't set up an abuse session. And my name is **not** Marie." The dip between her eyebrows and the pursing of her lips conveyed the rest of her message.

Ji-Yeong stepped fully in front of the lady blocking her completely from Jackass's view. Folding his arms across his chest, he stared down at the slightly shorter man.

"You heard the lady. She doesn't give her consent. So, you need to move along."

Flicking his fingers, he shooed Jackass Sinister away.

"Are you fucking serious right now?" He tried to look around Ji-Yeong to make eye contact with Beauty.

"Don't talk to her. She doesn't want to talk to you. Take a hint. Find a **willing** partner while you still can."

"What the fuck is that supposed to mean asshole?"

"Too late."

Ji-Yeong looked over the man's shoulder to the approaching club security. His glance alerted Sinister to their presence as well. Rotating toward them, Sinister put up his hands and changed his tune.

"Hey...Fellas. We're all good here. No problems."

Security ignored him and looked at Ji-Yeong who had zero issue letting them know what transpired. After a quick confirmation from Beauty, they escorted the sullen Sinister from the club. Ji-Yeong was sure the only thing keeping the jackass from causing a scene was the hope of his compliance—his quiet exit—would keep him from being banned from the club.

Claiming the seat next to Beauty at the bar, Ji-Yeong rotated the chair to face her. His eyes raked over her assessing her condition.

"Are you okay?"

Exhaling in a light whoosh, she nodded. "I'm fine. Just thinking maybe coming here was a mistake."

Ji-Yeong assumed a relaxed posture with his elbow on the bar top and his head resting against his fist. "Why do you think it was a mistake?

Because of that asshole?" He jerked his thumb in the direction security had taken Sinister.

"He's not the norm around here. Everyone knows better than to try the stunt he pulled. I don't know what he was thinking."

Beauty nodded, but he didn't think she was convinced, simply being polite. His draw to her wouldn't allow Ji-Yeong to turn back to his own drink. Extending his hand, he introduced himself with a slight smile.

"I'm Ji-Yeong. My friends call me Gee."

Returning the greeting and the smile, she replied, "I'm Maria."

"Very nice to meet you, Maria. Regardless of the circumstances."

"It's nice to meet you as well, Ji-Yeong."

Ji-Yeong's smile broadened. Not only had she not taken the bait to shorten his name to the more English sounding, Gee, but she'd pronounced his given name correctly. Granted, there was a slight southern lilt to it, but it was obvious she tried.

Leaning his forearm against the gleaming surface of the bar, Ji-Yeong captured her gaze smiling internally at the hint of shyness behind her hazel eyes.

"So, Maria. Considering where we are, I hope you don't think me too forward. But, what was that guy *supposed* to do to you? Or with you?"

Chapter Three

Maria stared into Ji-Yeong's chocolate-colored eyes and contemplated telling him to mind his business. After her brief encounter with the so-called Dom Tahlia set her up with, she wasn't sure she even wanted to be at Club Desire. Tahlia may have wasted her money on the membership fee.

When she opened her mouth to respond, the words she planned disappeared. In their place, was a sentence she'd had no intention to verbalize.

"I asked to be able to relinquish control. To have someone else be in charge. To allow me to fully receive pleasure and let go without fear of judgment."

With every fiber of her being, Maria wanted to clamp her hand over her mouth and snatch the runaway words back. Her eyes rounded into saucers as she managed to lock her lips over her teeth, stemming the confessional flow.

The slow smile spreading across Ji-Yeong's face was so sexy. The wings flapping in her stomach were more pterodactyl than butterfly in their fierceness. His lips inspired so many carnal thoughts. Her inner vixen sat up asking, *'What that mouth do?'*. Maria narrowly succeeded in keeping those words trapped inside.

The part of her which wanted to let loose and be free grew stronger the more time she spent in his presence. *What the hell was up with that?* She didn't know this man from a hole in the wall. How had he been able to climb inside her defenses in a matter of minutes?

It couldn't be alcohol, because she hadn't had any. Maybe it was the overall sensual vibe of the club. But, if it was the environment, why had she been completely turned off by Sinister?

Ji-Yeong's sinfully deep voice cut into her thoughts. Her center clenched in response, begging for a tete-a-tete. Seemingly, her lady bits were game to try to salvage the night. She'd started it with the resolve to step outside her comfort zone. Who said it had to end because it hadn't worked out with the person who was set to be her companion?

"If relinquishing control is your goal. I'm certain I can help you with that."

If Maria's eyes got any rounder, she'd turn into an owl. The shiver his declaration sent down her spine met up with the tingle in her nether regions resulting in the slickening of her walls. He spoke with such confidence; she believed every word. Her pussy was definitely campaigning for her to accept his offer. But...what was he offering?

Maria didn't want the night to be a bust. She'd flown in to spend the weekend letting loose and participating in debauchery for once in her life. Was she really going to throw in the towel after one not-so-pleasant encounter? An encounter Tahlia definitely would hear about later.

Fueled by her desire to see the experience through, and bolstered with the knowledge of the club being serious about safety, Maria tossed caution to the wind. Leaning against the bar with her cheek resting on her hand, she grinned at Ji-Yeong.

"Oh really? How would you help me?"

Maria squeaked when he reached beneath her seat and used the leg of the chair to scoot her closer to him. Once her knees were between his long legs, he stopped.

"There. That's better." Placing both hands where she could see them, he probed her with an intense stare. "Do I have your permission to touch you? Not sexually." The unspoken *not yet* hung between them.

Maria nodded, to which Ji-Yeong immediately shook his head no. "I need your words, Beauty."

Her breath hitched. He hadn't called her beautiful. He'd used the word beauty in place of her name. Like it had always been so. His sinfully sexy voice combined with his handsome face and the intensity of his stare almost made her forget there was a question requiring a response.

"Beauty? May I touch you?"

"Yes." Maria's reply was breathy. Her voice was foreign to her ears.

As soon as the word hit the air, Ji-Yeong's fingertips reached for the belt on the coat she still wore and tugged at the knot, loosening it. In keeping with her plan to let her hair down, Maria wore a figure hugging red Bodycon dress which stopped just above her knees.

She blamed the coolness of the lounge for her not taking the coat off prior to his non-verbal instructions. Her pulse kicked up as he slowly slid the garment down her shoulders and off her arms.

As he did, his fingertips skimmed along her arms leaving goosebumps in their wake. While he helped her with her coat, he spoke to her.

"Did you take the tour of the club? Bethany normally offers one to new members."

"I didn't. I expected my...date to show me around."

He nodded. Draping her coat over the back of his chair, he wrapped one hand around her wrist, tugging her forearm closer to him. Studying her face, he traced patterns on her skin.

"Okay. So, I'll give you a quick rundown. We'll get to know each other a little. Then we move on from there? Do you agree?"

Maria's head bobbed in agreement.

"Words, Beauty."

"Yes." The command in his voice called to a place in her that Maria had no idea even existed until tonight. It never crossed her mind to *not* adhere to his demand. Maria also had ceased to be concerned with how old or young he was. Ji-Yeong had pushed such thoughts completely from her mind with the big dick energy emanating from him.

"Good. The lounge is where we mingle. We decide if we are suitable for one another and want to play. If we both decide we want more, then we negotiate the terms of our play. Once we reach an agreement, we move on to the upper floors.

The second floor is for those with a...let's say have a penchant for voyeurism or exhibitionism. Or...Both. Whatever strikes your fancy. We don't judge here."

His eyes never left her face. Maria was certain he was gauging her non-verbal response to the information he supplied.

"If the second floor isn't your bag, there is a third floor. It is similar to the second floor, but it has rooms to afford more privacy for those who don't want to play in front of others. Any questions?"

Maria's focus was in and out due to the feel of his lightly callused fingertips skating along her skin. She caught enough of what he said to get the gist. Running the tip of her tongue across her lips, she noticed his eyes tracking the movement. His bottom lip disappeared between his teeth before he released it. *Good.* She wasn't the only one affected.

"Are you a Dom?"

"Good question." Ji-Yeong stopped his torture and tangled their fingers on one hand together on the bar top. The other rested on his thigh.

"I am a Dom, but my type is relatively new to the BDSM world. I'm what is known as a Pleasure Dom. Very similar to a Service Dom, but there are some differences."

Maria couldn't recall ever hearing of a Pleasure Dom in any of her research on the subject.

"Can you explain more?"

"Of course." Ji-Yeong's thumb began tracing a pattern on her palm. "A Pleasure Dom focuses on pleasing their partner. They take the time to learn what actions heighten the experience for their playmate and they endeavor to enhance it.

Depending on the person, it could involve edging...multiple orgasms...or complete orgasm denial. The primary goal of the Dom is to provide the most intense pleasure their partner can handle during their time together."

Maria couldn't say if it was his voice, the way his thumb stroked her palm, his description of a Pleasure Dom, or the deliberate way he relayed the information, but the warmth in her core had graduated to pulsing. Her lashes fluttered as she considered the possibilities.

In the past, she'd never been able to have just one night with a stranger. She felt so exposed during sex, it required a degree of trust which was hard to achieve with someone she didn't know well. The extensive questionnaire she filled out in advance of her date with Sinister made her think it might be possible in this environment, because of the advanced effort. With him, it couldn't work, but with Ji-Yeong...Maybe it could.

"So, Beauty. Tell me about your desires? Anything beyond being able to relinquish control? Are you interested in bondage? I'm not the sort of Dom who inflicts pain, but I'm willing to explore what brings you pleasure."

The way his lips moved and his voice dropped an octave when he said 'pleasure' had Maria on the verge of creaming her panties. *Who was this man and why did her body already want to bend to his will?*

From his explanation of a Pleasure Dom, he actually sounded more suitable to her fantasy than the other types of dominants she'd studied. While some aspects of the traditional Dom intrigued her, she wasn't sure she'd be able to give herself over to that type of experience completely. It took a great deal of trust.

Licking her lips again, she watched Ji-Yeong's gaze follow the movement. Then, she took a leap.

Chapter Four

Ji-Yeong studied Beauty's every expression and movement waiting for her reply. He was happy she consented to being touched since he had a difficult time keeping his hands to himself. He felt her pulse beating rapidly beneath his fingers. So, he knew he affected her.

The way her eyes widened and her pupils constricted were tell-tale signs of arousal. He desperately hoped she had the courage to continue. Whatever she chose, Ji-Yeong knew he wouldn't allow the night to end without connecting with her in some way. He didn't dwell on why it was so important for him to bond with this particular woman.

She was beautiful. Her body was a delicious combination of lush hips, round ass and heavy breasts. Add in the thick thighs and calves and he was surprised he was able to keep his tongue from hanging out of his mouth like an old school cartoon character.

Those things were wonderful, but physical attractiveness wasn't the only thing capable of moving him. Her vibe said he picked the perfect night to come to the club alone. He waited with bated breath for her response to his last question about her desires.

"I've never heard of a Pleasure Dom, but your description is intriguing."

"Does that mean you'll stay? Allow me to show you around and explore all the sexy things you've been too shy to admit out loud?"

"I'm not shy."

Ji-Yeong arched an eyebrow at her denial. After a few moments, she gifted him with a lopsided grin before squeezing his fingers.

"I'm not *shy*. Just reserved."

Nodding, he decided to let her have that one. "If you say so."

They spent the next several minutes talking. Being the type of Dominant he was, typically required a relatively close relationship or association with the Sub. It helped to understand his partner's desires, their tells, and their limits. Since he and Beauty had less than an hour of knowing one another under their belts, he'd have to approach their session differently.

While she had only agreed to exploring, he was banking on them actually making it to the third floor before the night was over. He began asking her basic questions. Making certain not to dwell on sexual history, he learned she worked a high-powered, stressful job.

When he considered the way she carried herself, it fit. She exuded confidence. Her gaze held an alertness of everything happening around her as if she were calculating how to respond in any given situation. She also hinted at having to maintain a certain image all the time. Doing so didn't lend itself to being carefree and adventurous.

It sounded tortuous to Ji-Yeong. He resolved to be the person she could release with—the place where her image and obligations held no bearing on their interactions. He couldn't wait to strip away her polished exterior to reach the passionate woman he knew rested just beneath the surface.

Their dialogue wasn't entirely focused on her. She asked him questions as well. He had no problem letting her in on aspects of his life he'd previously refused to discuss with his playmates. His oversharing, should've clued him in that Beauty was more than just another plaything.

Ji-Yeong's parents had immigrated to the United States prior to his birth. So, while he was born in the U.S., in many ways, he'd been raised traditionally Korean. His parents had become more flexible over the years. But they didn't ease off until he developed his first Application—which turned him into a millionaire overnight. He was nineteen, and their only child.

It took an unbelievable amount of parental guilt and negotiations to convince him finishing college would benefit him. To get them off his back, he finished in three years instead of four. At which point, he immediately married his college sweetheart and they had their first and only child together—his son Ryu. The marriage was a disaster, as expected since they both were so young and admittedly selfish.

But they loved their son and worked together to give him a good life. They were co-parenting long before the term became popular. Turned out, he and Min were much better friends than life partners. She was now married to a software engineer and living in Seattle. Ryu was in his freshman year of college in California.

Ji-Yeong didn't reveal all of that to Beauty, but he did tell her about his business ventures which somewhat intersected with hers. After his first App sale, he developed a few more and began investing in various industries. He wouldn't consider himself an Angel Investor, but he'd gotten in on a couple of small ventures before they blew up, netting him enough for him to provide for himself, his parents and his son for several lifetimes.

"So, you have your fingers in a little bit of everything?"

He nodded in response to her question, but his mind was already on what he'd like to have his fingers in next. The thought brought a lopsided grin to his face.

"Now that we have gotten to know each other a bit, are you ready to establish some ground rules?"

The mention of rules caused her to sit up straighter and alter her relaxed demeanor. He couldn't have her withdrawing from him. Retaking her hand, he laced their fingers together.

"Hey...No need to put on your business face. We need to talk guidelines for both of our safety. This is the unsexy part of things, but I promise to guide us through it as efficiently as possible."

She released a sigh and her shoulders relaxed a little. Ji-Yeong took it as a win. He'd already determined how he wanted to approach her introduction, but her consent was required for them to move forward.

"Any hard limits? Things you know for sure you don't want?"

"No bodily fluids."

Her response was immediate and delivered with a shudder denoting how she felt on the subject. He didn't blame her, with the exception of one particular bodily fluid.

"All...bodily fluids?" When he tilted his head and lifted one eyebrow she got his message.

"Let me clarify. No piss, shit, or spitting on me. No cum in my face, but other areas we can negotiate."

Ji-Yeong appreciated her bluntness, but the mention of his cum on her —anywhere—had his cock plumping in his pants faster than an inflatable emergency raft. Picturing her supple brown skin coated in his essence was a visual he couldn't shake. Making the image a reality became a new goal.

"I can work with that. What about pain?"

"I thought you didn't do pain."

"I don't, with the exception of light spankings." Ji-Yeong couldn't prevent his voice from deepening. When he mentioned spanking, his hand tingled with the desire to connect to her rounded ass, testing how it would bounce at the contact.

He didn't miss the way her breathing hitched when he offered spanking as an option. His Beauty was intrigued at the thought. He gathered her previous lovers hadn't gone there with her. Ji-Yeong liked the idea of being her first.

"Can we." She cleared her throat, and her fingers gripped his slightly. "Can we play that part by ear?"

"Of course." Unable to help himself, he cupped the side of her face with his other hand. Her skin was the finest of silks beneath his touch.

"Now, on to the last couple of items before we move upstairs. I normally use the stop light method for determining if we should keep going. Red means stop. Yellow means pause or slow down. And green means you're okay to continue. Do you agree with the system?"

Initially, she nodded, but Ji-Yeong's expression prompted her to vocalize her agreement. "Yes. I agree."

"Good. Do you have a safe word?"

"Do we need one?"

"Absolutely. Any type of play requires something to bring an immediate halt to all activities. Saying 'red' only stops the scene momentarily. Using your safe word stops all play for the session. It means you can't take any more."

"If we aren't doing rough stuff, I wonder why it's necessary. You make it sound like you intend to have me cumming so hard I'll want to tap out."

Leaning in until his nose almost touched hers, Ji-Yeong narrowed her vision to only his eyes. "Beauty, it is necessary because your complete and utter sensual surrender is my mission. If I don't make you come so hard you can't fathom going on a moment longer, I'm not doing my job correctly."

Ji-Yeong took great enjoyment in watching her eyes widen then flutter closed at his statement. He meant every word. His plan was to drain many mind-altering orgasms from his Beauty as possible before she threw in the towel. His cock throbbed in anticipation of their play.

"Um...Okay then. Foreclosure. My safe word is Foreclosure."

"Is that a word you think you can remember while in distress?" He didn't want to scare her, but the word sounded so obscure, Ji-Yeong had to be certain.

"Yes. I'll remember."

"Foreclosure it is."

Sitting up straight, he stood from his seat. Grabbing her coat, he extended his arm to her. They checked her coat at the coat check. Then, he escorted her to the elevator which would take them to the second floor. He wouldn't usher her directly to the third floor. Not just yet. He wanted to gauge her reaction to the scene being played out on the raised dais. If he wasn't mistaken, Hinata and Valentina were supposed to do a Shibari scene tonight.

Chapter Five

Maria hoped she projected the confidence she wanted to feel in the moment. For the most part, Ji-Yeong had made her comfortable with the idea, but there was still an undercurrent of nervousness. *What if he wasn't as attracted to her once she disrobed?*

No man, other than Oscar, had seen her naked in over twenty-five years. A lot had changed since she was twenty-nine and childless. Her breasts were still full, but they didn't sit up perkily on her chest. There was a pudginess to her stomach that refused to go away no matter how much she worked out. And she was more than a little generously curved in other areas.

She tried to shake the thoughts away as Ji-Yeong visually devoured her making it clear he liked what he saw. Clothed. What about naked? Maria's moment of self-doubt melted away when the elevator doors opened and they stepped out onto the second floor of Club Desire.

The sounds and sight of sex immediately captured her attention leaving no room for her to think about anything other than the hedonistic displays surrounding her. Her pulse quickened. The heat of Ji-Yeong's hand at the small of her back added to the rush of warmth to her center.

Other than the occasional foray into viewing adult films online, Maria had never considered herself a voyeur. Yet she couldn't tear her eyes away from the couples in various stages of coitus on the low couches and chairs throughout the room.

So caught up, she didn't initially notice not everyone was actively having sex. Some had their gazes trained in a particular direction. Following the path of their stares, she saw a couple on a raised dais toward the back of the room opposite the bar.

A woman lay on the bed. Well... Maria subconsciously tilted her head to one side. It was more like she was trussed up. Intricately. With rope. A tall, handsome man with prominent Asian features stood beside the bed stroking his length. Had it not been for Ji-Yeong guiding her through the room, she was certain she would've been rooted in the spot just inside the entryway.

When he located a place for them to sit, she didn't bother to look behind her. Taking his encouragement, she lowered herself onto the plush surface. The brush of Ji-Yeong's firm body settling next to hers added an additional layer to the arousal simmering in her core.

"Do you like that, Beauty? Does it intrigue you?"

Ji-Yeong's words tickled her ears due to his closeness. The kiss he planted on her bare shoulder sent an uncontrollable shiver through her. His chuckle told her he'd noticed her response, and the tightening of the hand he rested on her thigh said he enjoyed the affect he had on her.

Words escaped her as Maria watched the man on the stage trace his fingers along the areas of skin exposed by the ropes he'd bound around his partner. The woman's legs were spread, with her knees bracketing her chest—being held apart by the rope somehow. The position left her pussy exposed.

Both arms were secured to her sides. Her pebbled nipples peeked through the binding around her breasts. The man flicked his pointer finger over one turgid peak before capturing it between his finger and thumb, pinching it.

Maria wasn't sure how much or how little pressure he used, but the result was the woman's head dropping back onto the bed and her body arching as much as it could into his touch. A guttural moan tore from her throat. Desire pooled in Maria's stomach at the unexpected sensuality of the scene.

Shifting her thighs, she squirmed as she shared the unknown woman's pleasure even though she hadn't felt the man's touch. Their connection pulsed with a life of its own. It was palpable.

Electric impulses skated beneath the surface of Maria's skin when Ji-Yeong pressed his lips close to her ear again.

"Do I have your permission to touch you, Beauty?"

Maria's 'yes' was released in a raspy rush. The sensual energy between them was elevated by the display on the dais and the erotic sounds of coupling not five feet from where they sat.

Ji-Yeong's long, nimble fingers mimicked the actions of the man on the stage. He caressed her breast, then circled her nipple. The material of her dress and the thin lace of her bra were no deterrent to him locating his target. Maria wanted to close her eyes to savor the feeling, but she didn't want to cut off the sight of the couple.

The man praised the woman. Calling her a good girl, he said she'd earned a reward. The woman's eyes blazed with need as she stared at his erection mere inches from her face. The man stroked it, moving closer to her lips. Then, at the last moment, he spun her around, dropped to his knees and buried his face between her spread legs, lapping at her pussy.

The pterodactyl wings were back in Maria's stomach, watching the unknown man devouring his partner's essence. The woman's body visibly trembled and her eyes rolled back into her head. Ji-Yeong had confirmed not all BDSM scenes involved actual sex. But, Maria couldn't imagine going through something so titillating without completing the deed. As it was, she was ruining her underwear just observing.

Maria didn't know if the moan she released was in commiseration with the woman on the stage or because Ji-Yeong's hand had slipped beneath the edge of her dress. His wide palm and long fingers rubbed her thigh in an upward trajectory, stopping millimeters shy of her weeping core.

"Do I have your permission to touch your pussy, Beauty?"

Ji-Yeong's request dripped over Maria's skin like warm honey. Words were difficult, but he didn't move a muscle until a strangled 'yes' tumbled from her lips. The moment it did, her panties were pushed to the side. With a dexterity that would impress a surgeon, he found her pearl, worrying the bundle of nerves and drawing breathy moans from her lips.

The man on the stage dipped his tongue inside the woman's channel.

Ji-Yeong dipped one finger inside Maria's slick walls, continuing to mimic the erotic display before them. Maria's bottom lip disappeared between her teeth as she fought against loudly crying out from all the stimulation.

Ji-Yeong was right there in her ear to offer encouragement.

"Don't hide your pleasure, Beauty. Let them hear it. It turns them on to hear the sound of your desire."

He ended his statement by kissing along the column of her neck. She tilted her head to the side to give him better access while keeping her eyes glued to the actions on the stage. Her eyelids fluttered and almost closed when Ji-Yeong made his way back to her ear.

"Do I have your permission to suck your titties, Beauty? Your nipples are so hard. They're begging for my attention."

Despite the heat banked behind his dark eyes, Ji-Yeong shook his head when she only offered a nod in reply. He didn't verbalize his demand for her words. His expression conveyed the message for him.

"Yes, you can suck them, kiss, them, touch them. Please, Ji-Yeong."

Maria had never been so sexually stimulated in her life. It was as if she and Ji-Yeong existed in a bubble. They were submerged in lust, apart from the others in the lounge. But she was able to view their acts through a periscope. She vaguely heard Ji-Yeong's chuckle as he tugged at the vee at the neckline of her dress exposing one breast.

She couldn't bring herself to care if anyone saw them when his lips closed around her nipple, giving it a suckling kiss before clamping his teeth around the sensitive peak. Simultaneously, he added another finger stretching her walls around his thick digits. When he rotated them finding the elusive spot inside her, she could no longer maintain her gaze on the scene in front of her.

Her eyelids slammed closed. Fireworks exploded behind them and she was tossed into an orgasm so strong she lost control of her limbs. The entire time Ji-Yeong had been conducting his pleasurable assault, her hands had been fisted against the cushions of the Lover's Chair.

Her nails scrapped against the fabric as she fought against losing control. Ji-Yeong had proven her fight to be a futile effort. The combination of his ministrations, the mewls and moans of those around them, and the cries of the bound woman on the dais were enough to drive her to the edge. All he had to do was breathe to push her over.

A stinging sensation radiated from her nipple before soft pecks were applied. Ji-Yeong kissed a path back up the column of her neck.

"What did I tell you about hiding your pleasure, Beauty? I want your cries. Your screams of completion are the platinum hits that I dream about. I *will* have them."

Ji-Yeong growled his declaration into her ear as he removed his fingers from her still quivering pussy. Maria's lids lifted to half-mast and she turned her head to look at him. His eyes were waiting for hers, filled with promises about what was to come. She watched as he placed the fingers, coated with her essence, into his mouth.

Maintaining their visual connection, he licked them clean. The way his tongue moved around his digits and his lashes lowered to his cheeks in enjoyment, she had an image of what he might look like savoring her juices directly from the source. The thought caused a resurgence in her core.

Any lingering hesitation was gone. Maria was ready to take things to the next level. If his abilities only got better from this point, she was certain she would end the night in a state of unimaginable satisfaction. She'd considered cursing Tahlia out for the Sinister debacle, but after what she'd just experienced with Ji-Yeong, she might have to thank her friend instead.

Chapter Six

Although Ji-Yeong saw desire etched across her face and he was ninety-nine-point nine-nine percent certain of what she wanted, he still asked the question.

"Are you ready to go to a room now, Beauty?"

Maria's sluggish nod was accompanied by a clear 'yes'. Ji-Yeong took pride in knowing he'd brought her such enjoyment when he had yet to use his best moves.

Despite not having picked a partner before he arrived, Ji-Yeong had reserved a room to play. He was happy he'd had such foresight. Guiding Beauty through the writhing bodies on the second floor, it took significant control for him to maintain an easy pace.

There was no need to rush, but he was eager to be alone with her. He hadn't missed the moment of doubt she'd had in the elevator. She probably thought she hid it well, but he'd picked up on it. He couldn't wait to show her that it was impossible for him to be disappointed.

The only way he'd be dissatisfied was if she called an end to everything before he got the chance to show her how great they could be together. Even then, he would just devise a plan to keep them in each other's orbit.

When they stepped off the elevator on the third floor, Ji-Yeong's gaze was glued to Maria's face. He watched as she visually devoured the even more sensual debauchery of this level of the club. She was transfixed staring at the dancers in the cages suspended from the ceiling.

Male and female dancers twirled and gyrated in the gilded cages under the red ambient glow of the lounge. The pulsating music added to the decadent feel. As much as he wanted to allow her to explore, he was driven to continue their session in a private setting.

She'd allowed some liberties downstairs, but he was certain she hadn't let go enough for her to do the things he had planned in front of others. Gliding his fingertips along her arm, he drew her attention to him. He tangled their digits together. Tipping his head toward the hallway to the left of the elevator, he tugged gently.

"This way, Beauty."

Ji-Yeong chuckled to himself at the way she looked into the room until it was no longer possible to see inside. Then, she turned her attention to the fixtures in the hallway. The corridor itself was pretty non-descript. It could be a normal hotel, except *normal* hotels didn't tend to stock their rooms with toys at the request of their guests.

At least Ji-Yeong wasn't aware of a hotel which would supply nipple clamps, vibrators, cock rings and floggers. Not that he'd encountered in his extensive travels. Specialty establishments had entire packages designed for satisfying a couples' pleasure. He'd encountered those primarily during his visits to European countries.

Once they crossed the threshold into the room he'd reserved, Ji-Yeong saw he'd made a mistake. He hadn't continued the touches and caresses needed to keep Beauty tethered to the moment. It had been an act of self-preservation. Had he continued to stimulate her, he would've temporarily lost sight of providing her the experience he promised.

He'd required the time to collect himself. But, collecting himself had given her the opportunity to come out of the lustful fog she'd happily slipped into in the second-floor lounge. Her gaze flit around the room. Wrapping his arms around her, he pulled her back to his front.

Beauty was average height. However, her heels gave her enough lift to keep him from having to lean down very far to nuzzle the crook of her neck and speak into her ear.

"Are you okay?"

When she didn't immediately respond he prompted. "It's fine if you're not. But I can't fix it, if I don't know what's wrong."

After a few beats she spoke. "It's just...I know what I saw downstairs, and I know what I agreed to...Seeing this room. Hearing the door close and lock behind me...It made everything real. I didn't expect it to hit me like that."

Ji-Yeong tightened his hold briefly, giving her the hug she needed, but hadn't asked for.

"I understand. Don't worry. We'll go as slow or as fast as you want."

Her hair brushed against the side of his face when she nodded. Reluctantly, he released her from his embrace. Walking over to the console opposite the large bed, he fingered the items laying on top of it. Looking back at her, he extended his hand.

"Come, Beauty. I want to show you something."

Ji-Yeong studied her as she approached slowly. He watched as her gaze flit over the large bed with its crimson bed coverings. The posts at each corner of the bed were sturdy and connected to a canopy. The sheer fabric panels attached to the canopy were tied back strategically to give the effect of partial exposure, adding to the erotic theme of the space. The low, pulsating beat of the music coming from the hidden speakers supplied another sensual layer.

When Maria reached his side, he positioned her in front of him facing the console. Before them was a collection of toys and implements. The majority of which were designed to heighten a woman's pleasure during sex. There were a few things designed for men as well. However, since he derived the most gratification from pleasing his partner, there weren't many.

"What's all this?"

"What does it look like?"

Chuckling, Ji-Yeong nuzzled the crook of her neck. She smelled so delicious, he couldn't help himself.

"A bunch of sex toys." Reaching out, she picked up the beginner anal plug still in the packaging. Holding it aloft, she looked up at him.

"I know what it's for, but what are your intentions with this?"

Lifting it from her fingers, he replaced the plug next to the corresponding graduated plug.

"*We* are going to do whatever it is you want to do with it. If you don't want to use these, we won't."

Nodding, her hand hovered over the other items like she was shopping for fine jewelry. There was actually jewelry present. It just wasn't the kind typically worn in public.

"That's good to know. I'm still game to explore, but I'm not quite so adventurous tonight."

Ji-Yeong wanted to say they had time to explore it another day, but he locked the words in his throat. He was aware of how much enjoyment some women derived from anal sex, but it wasn't everyone's thing. There were plenty of other paths open and holes available for their carnal use.

Her fingers grazed a package and he waited in anticipation of her actually opening it or at least inquiring about the contents. Maria put him out of his misery when she opened the closure at the top and tipped the contents into her hand. When she held it up, the function of the long silver chain wasn't easily recognizable.

He wondered if she realized she hummed to herself as she inspected the piece. Refusing to break the silence, he waited for either the question or statement of recognition. A sharp inhale followed her flicking one of the clamps dangling from the chain.

"Wait...Why are there three? No. Don't answer that." Quickly, but gently, she returned the chain with the nipple and clit clamps back to the see-through pouch.

"I take it we will not be using those tonight either." Ji-Yeong placed his hands on her hips aligning her luscious ass with his crotch.

"Am I disappointing you?"

Using her hips to turn her around, he captured her gaze.

"Hey. This isn't about me. Remember your pleasure is my pleasure. So, we won't do anything you aren't comfortable with. We can keep this as vanilla as you like, or we can venture out and test your limits."

Cupping her cheeks in his hands, he tilted her chin up. "You have the power here, Beauty. Everything we do will be consensual and geared toward your enjoyment. Now...While I've had many partners who loved using any number of these toys, we don't have to use *any* of them to achieve my goal of bringing you the ultimate pleasure."

Above all, Ji-Yeong wanted her to be comfortable and feel as if she could trust him. If she didn't. If she couldn't. Nothing would happen tonight, and he would have to be okay with that. *God he hoped not.*

Ghosting a thumb across her lips, he allowed himself a minute to admire their fullness. Lifting his gaze back to hers he searched her eyes for the answers he sought. Returning to her lips, he groaned internally. He had to taste them.

"Do I have your permission to kiss you, Beauty?"

Maria's lashes fluttered, she inhaled slightly before she nodded. "Yes."

Her word was swallowed by his lips as he took hers in a scorching kiss. *Damn.* They felt even better than they looked. When she provided an opening, he delved his tongue inside seeking her flavor.

Chapter Seven

Regardless of her slight bout of uncertainty concerning the situation, the moment Ji-Yeong's lips touched hers, flames licked across Maria's skin. They blazed a path to her center causing her Kegel muscles to clench as if he was already inside her. Or was it in memory of the way he'd skillfully used his fingers to bring her to orgasm just minutes before?

The moans she released were captured by his kisses and returned with caresses. Maria loved the way his hands felt on her body. They were so large, they almost made her generous curves feel exactly the right size to fit them.

"Do I have your permission to remove your clothes, Beauty?"

Fuck! The way he called her Beauty when he asked a question never failed to bring her to the brink of creaming her panties. His voice was a weapon he wielded with proficiency. How had he managed to lace sexual innuendo into such a simple phrase as *'Do I have your permission'*? Each time he said the words, she wanted to submit in whatever way necessary to obtain the promise behind the question.

"Yes!" Maria was certain her response was what people were talking about when they said enthusiastic consent was required.

Ji-Yeong's fingers dragged across her collarbone as he tugged the straps of her dress and bra from her shoulders. Tingling preceded the goosebumps following in the wake of his touch. Once the straps rested at her elbows and the cool air of the room hit her breasts, he'd relocated them to the bed. Her bra lay discarded along their path.

Seated with her standing between his legs, he licked his lips while staring at her full, heavy globes. Any thought that he'd be turned off upon seeing her naked were abandoned with the hungry way he looked at her. Those chocolate eyes met hers displaying his desire bluntly.

"Do I have your permission to worship your body, Beauty? May I suck your tits and taste the sweetness of your pussy from the source?"

Maria swayed with the power of her need. She tried to say yes, but only a hoarse croak left her lips. The imagery his request evoked stole her voice and all she wanted to do was feel. Without the ability to verbalize, she did the next best thing. She buried her fingers in his hair and tugged his head to her breast.

Maybe actions *were* an acceptable answer, because Ji-Yeong immediately latched onto one nipple. Maria's knees nearly buckled from the sensation of his tongue flicking the turgid peak as he held it clamped between his teeth. Releasing it with a pop, he kissed his way up her chest while continuing to move her dress down and over her hips.

"Beauty, you aren't adhering to the rules. Are you trying to be punished?"

Why did the possibility of punishment sound so good when promised in Ji-Yeong's baritone voice? Maria didn't know, but she was tempted to purposely rebel just to find out. Instead, she somehow located her voice.

"Yes."

Ji-Yeong's hands stilled in the motion of sliding her panties off over her ass.

"Yes, what? Are you trying to be punished?"

"No. Yes."

"Which is it, Beauty?"

Gritting her teeth in frustration. Maybe she wasn't a big enough girl for the kind of play Ji-Yeong offered. She couldn't seem to get her shit together. Taking a deep breath, she tried not to think about how close his face was to her dripping pussy and how his hands felt resting against the rounded cheeks of her ass.

"No...I don't want to be punished. And, yes you have my permission to suck my titties, kiss my pussy, touch me wherever you want, do whatever you think I'll like."

Maria sought to get the formalities out of the way. Her thought was to use her safe word if he stepped out of bounds. But, from the shaking of Ji-Yeong's head, he wasn't having it.

"No, Beauty. I won't accept permissions I haven't requested yet. No shortcuts."

Resuming his removal of her clothing, he tapped each calf for her to step out of the dress before removing her shoes. Maria wanted to stomp her feet at his deliberate motions, but she couldn't deny the sensuality of having a man carefully undress her with the sole purpose of wringing every ounce of pleasure from her body.

Once she was nude, Ji-Yeong switched their positions. After ripping away the expensive looking duvet, he seated her on the bed, spread her legs and dropped to his knees between them. Ravenous was the only way to describe the way he looked at her. If she held even a microscopic hint of self-doubt, his expression flicked it away.

"Lay back, baby. I believe I was given permission to worship your body and taste your sweet pussy."

Maria made contact with the cool sheets at the same time Ji-Yeong tossed her legs over his shoulders and dove face first into her weeping snatch. Her back bowed so hard, she thought she heard it crack. *This man knew what the fuck he was doing!*

His movements weren't tentative. It was like he held a roadmap, no a pussy map, if you will. He located her spots with such precision, Maria felt like he'd spent years instead of minutes learning the things she liked. He responded to each moan, inhale, hip tilt and finger flex that she made.

Without thought, her digits delved into his hair, wrapping around the silky straight strands. His inky hair was just long enough for her to get a decent grip. She raked her fingernails lightly over his scalp drawing a moan which sent vibrations through her sensitive folds. Maria's chest heaved trying to take in air. She was already on the verge of cumming again.

Abruptly, Ji-Yeong's heavenly tongue and lips ceased their worship. His hands landed on hers tugging her digits from his hair. The noise torn from her throat was a cross between a moan and a growl.

"What? Why did you stop?"

"Trust me, Beauty."

Rising from his position on the floor, he kissed a path up her thighs, over her stomach, stopping briefly at her breasts before ending at her lips. One quick peck was all he delivered before he pinned her with his serious gaze.

"What is your color?"

Maria frowned in confusion. "Huh?"

"What is your color? Have you forgotten the system already?"

His prompting lifted the lustful fog enough for the memory to take root. Gripping his sides, she tilted her hips against the bulge in his slacks.

"Green. Definitely green."

"That's good."

With a swiftness which made her head spin, Ji-Yeong stood from the bed and began shedding his clothes. Maria initially wanted to scream when he broke their connection. But as more of his lean muscular physique was revealed, she got lost in appreciating every inch of skin he exposed.

"Scoot back onto the bed, Beauty. Put your head on the pillow."

Maria followed his instruction without comment. The command in his voice didn't leave room for dispute—despite his assurance that she held the power. When his pants hit the floor, her pulse kicked up another notch at the bulge in his boxer briefs. Wetness gathered in her mouth when he lowered the band of his underwear and his long, thick shaft came into view. *Dios Mio.*

With his length swinging between his thighs, Ji-Yeong joined her on the bed. Her core clenched in anticipation of finally being filled. No thought was given as she spread her legs and reached for him. When he lay beside her on the sheets instead of pressing her body into the bed the way she wanted, Maria couldn't stop her pout from forming.

"Tsk...Beauty. You may have the power, but you don't get to control my methods for pleasing you. As much as I want to sink my cock inside your tight pussy, I can tell you haven't let go enough."

Maria wanted to object, she really did, but Ji-Yeong cupped one breast in his hand and covered her areola, tugging her nipple into his mouth. Not neglecting the other breast, he pinched it between his thumb and forefinger, twisting with the perfect amount of pressure. The throbbing in her core started up again with a vengeance.

She could come from the attention he gave her breasts alone, but she wanted the thickness leaking on her thigh inside her when she had her next orgasm. The desire became so overwhelming, Maria began to beg. At this point, she had no shame. She simply wanted Ji-Yeong inside her.

"Please. Please, Ji-Yeong. Please just fuck me."

Ji-Yeong groaned around her breast before releasing it. He pulled back to look into her face. Her hands followed him rubbing his chest and reaching for the velvet wrapped steel between his legs.

"You are a rule breaker. I should punish you, but...Fuck!" Seemingly from nowhere, he produced a condom rolling it onto his length. In seconds he was on his knees with his hands pressing her thighs toward her chest. His dick poised at the entrance to her channel.

"Do I have your permission to fuck this tight pussy, Beauty?"

Didn't she just beg him to do just that?

"Yes! Please, yes! Green! Green!"

Maria's chanting became a keening wail as Ji-Yeong fed his length into her starving channel. He stretched her so deliciously; it was impossible for her to do anything beyond take strangled breaths.

He didn't stop until they were pelvis to pelvis with his thickness completely inside her slick walls. Fire blazed behind his eyes as he looked down at her.

"You got your way this time, Beauty. I'm going to fuck you to orgasm the way you want. Next round, you'll pay for pushing me like this."

Maria didn't have the will nor capacity to argue his point. Ji-Yeong's hips began a stroking rhythm which wiped away any thoughts beyond how wonderful he felt inside her.

Chapter Eight

He'd lost control. Ji-Yeong knew it, but couldn't seem to bring himself to care. With Maria's heat wrapped around his length, he was barely able to keep himself from spilling into the condom on the first stroke. She fit him like a custom-made glove.

For the first time in years, he wished there wasn't a barrier between him and his partner. The thought caused a hitch in his motion, but he recovered delivering deep thrusts. Ji-Yeong couldn't fathom why a woman as desirable has Maria would need to set up a random encounter at a sex club. But, he'd never been more grateful he'd decided on a last-minute trip to Chicago.

Soft hands grasped Ji-Yeong's forearms and his gaze lifted from watching where they were joined to her beautiful face. It was flushed with a slight sheen of perspiration on her brow. He searched her expression for any signs of discomfort. She was causing him to toss out all of the rules, but one he wouldn't break or even bend was putting his partner's pleasure first.

"What's your color, Beauty?"

Maria moaned before releasing a lust filled, "green...mmm...yes. Green..."

Spreading her legs farther apart, he dropped over her in traditional missionary with his arms bracketing her head. Lowering his face to hers, he seized her full attention.

"Green?"

"Mmm. Yes. Green."

Fire burned Ji-Yeong's lower back as he restrained himself from plunging inside her unfettered. His hips gave a rough jerk in defiance of his control. Maria gasped in response as her walls fluttered around his cock.

"Did you like that?"

"Yes..."

Kissing her lips lightly, he blazed a trail across her jawline until he reached her ear.

"Do I have your permission to pound this pussy? Can you handle it? Would it please you to take my cock like that?"

Before she answered, her pussy clamped around his dick. The effect was like her channel was literally trying to suck him in deeper.

"Yes! I would be so very pleased, sir."

Fuck! He hadn't asked her to call him 'sir'. He never demanded it of any of his partners. Until now, it had simply been a word. Coming from his Beauty's lips, it was a galvanizing trigger. Ji-Yeong had minimal control of the way his hips dipped and swiveled drawing sounds of delight from Maria.

Her hands roamed his back before latching on to his buttocks. His cheeks contracted and relaxed with each thrust of his hips. Leveraging himself back to his knees, he maintained their connection. He could tell from her breathing, his Beauty was close. Ji-Yeong wasn't far behind her, but he was determined that she went before him.

Never a person to think one method worked for everyone, he had no problems seeking out her clit. Using his thumb, he massaged just to the right of it, not putting pressure directly on the little bundle of nerves. Almost immediately the quivering of her channel increased.

As much as he enjoyed watching his cock being swallowed by her magnificent pussy, Ji-Yeong was certain she was teetering on the edge of orgasm. Rotating his thumb in another firm circle, he flicked her pearl.

"Come for me, Beauty. Drench my cock in your sweet juices."

"Ah!"

Maria's exclamation was followed by a string of Spanglish which almost made Ji-Yeong blush. The combination of the way her velvet walls milked his cock and her uninhibited words pulled him over the brink with her. His thrusts became erratic jerks as he spilled his seed into the condom.

"Fuck...Beauty..."

Ji-Yeong lowered Maria's legs, settling between them. Keeping most of his weight off her body, he peppered kisses on her chest, making his way to her lips. The mating of their tongues was languid and devoid of the urgency from moments before. However, it didn't lack the ability to reignite the flame between them.

"Dios Mio. What are you doing to me?"

Her voice was scratchy and slightly hoarse drawing a cocky smirk from Ji-Yeong. She hadn't held back on volume when she let her string of Spanglish dirty talk go. Who would've thought his Beauty even knew such words?

"I'm keeping my word."

Ji-Yeong pecked her lips. Smoothing her hair back from her brow, he smiled at the drugged look on her face. His erection hadn't fully softened. He knew with a few strokes it would be hard as granite again. When he flexed his hips, he noticed her slight grimace before she wiped it away.

Unable to resist, he kissed her plump lips again as he withdrew from her honied haven and rolled to the side. She needed a break, and he needed to dispose of the condom.

Leaving the bed, he strolled into the ensuite bathroom. It didn't take him long to get the room ready, then he returned to find Maria curled onto her side facing him. Her hazel gaze was partially hidden behind her lashes. Her hands were folded together and tucked beneath the pillow. She looked like a well fucked woman. But Ji-Yeong wasn't done with her.

Stopping at the side of the bed, he extended his hand. "Come with me."

A line appeared between her eyebrows. "Where are we going? I don't think I can move yet."

Suppressing a smile Ji-Yeong simply stared at her with his hand extended. For the briefest moment, it appeared she was going to go full brat. Then, she accepted his hand allowing him to tug her upright. Once she was seated on the edge of the bed, he scooped her into his arms and stalked toward the bathroom.

"Ooo! Well! You should have led with the offer to carry me."

Ji-Yeong gave her a sideways glance.

"If I'd offered to carry you, tell me you wouldn't have said some shit about being too heavy."

Maria's mouth opened then closed without releasing a sound. The corner of his lips tipped up.

"Yeah. That's what I thought."

When they entered the bathroom, the scent of the rosemary and lemongrass essential oils met them. He'd put the oils in the bath to help sooth her sore muscles. By no means was their night over, but Ji-Yeong was no fool. It was obvious it had been a while for her. She'd need additional care to be able to withstand the marathon of pleasure he wanted to give her. Placing her on her feet next to the tub, he held on to her until he was certain she was steady.

"Wait one moment, Beauty."

Ji-Yeong went to the vanity to retrieve the brand-new brush and hair elastic. Her hair had been thoroughly mussed and the style no longer resembled the orderly curls she'd swept up off her nape with hair pins. Who the hell knew where the hairpins were at this point?

His gaze held hers in the mirror behind the custom tub as he approached her with his tools. When he was close, she partially turned toward him with her hand out. Ji-Yeong was aware what he planned could go either way. There were rules regarding touching a black woman's hair —especially without permission. But, caring for her was his responsibility. At least it was for the remainder of the night, or whenever they called a halt to their session.

He held the brush and elastic in one hand and away from Maria. She frowned in response. Her confusion was evident.

"Are you not going to allow me to care for you?" Ji-Yeong held her gaze, waiting for her reply.

"I didn't say that. It's thoughtful of you to have things which can be used to manage my hair. In my opinion that's part of caring for me."

Although she didn't say it, her statement implied no one else had thought of doing what he considered a bare minimum task. Ji-Yeong stepped closer to her, dipping his head near her face.

"Beauty, you will learn my definition of caring for you isn't such a low bar. When I say it, I mean you don't lift a finger. I provide your needs. You aren't required to even expend brain power to wonder how or when something will happen. Just know I'll handle it."

"What you're saying involves a great deal of trust."

"I'm aware."

They stared at one another for extended seconds before Maria gave the tiniest of nods. It resembled the tick of someone torn between standing firm while wanting desperately to relinquish control. His goal was to have Maria let go with the confidence that he could and would catch her, and deliver on every promise made.

Ji-Yeong pounced on the brief moment of acquiescence. "Do I have your permission to brush your hair?"

Questions swirled in her eyes as he patiently waited for her response. Finally, she rotated back toward the mirror with her gaze locked on their reflection.

"Yes."

Her answer was firm, but Ji-Yeong still approached slowly. Slipping the elastic onto one wrist, he began gently brushing the tangles at the end of her hair working his way to the scalp. Her coils were so soft, he almost got lost in feeling the strands wrapping around his fingers as he gathered her hair into a pineapple atop her head. When he was done, he placed a soft kiss to the base of her neck. Collecting himself he helped her into the tub.

Chapter Nine

"Watch your step. This tub is deeper than normal."

Maria nodded in response to Ji-Yeong's warning. He guided her into the tub which was perfectly capable of holding at least five pretty good-sized adults. There were textured stairs leading down into the scented water.

Once Maria stepped fully into the knee-high water, Ji-Yeong joined her. Although she knew her sweet spot couldn't handle another round just yet, she couldn't stop herself from watching his length bob in front of him. Even flaccid, it was impressive. Knowing it lengthened and thickened when fully erect had her lady bits tingling, encouraging her to take another ride. Who knew when she'd experience such a gifted lover again?

After he stepped behind her in the tub, he guided them to one side where he sat on a low ledge, tugging her down to sit between his legs. Maria had no complaints when she was fully immersed with her back pressed against his chest—although his penis being cradled against her lower back was slightly distracting.

"How are you feeling?"

Ji-Yeong's hands ghosted over her arms and down her sides with light touches before he brought them back up to her shoulders. A sigh left

Maria's lips without conscious thought. Taking his question seriously, she paused to consider the state of her body—her intimate bits specifically.

"I'm okay. It's a good thing I keep a regular exercise regimen though." She looked up over her shoulder at him. "If I didn't, we might've had to stop because I caught a Charlie Horse."

She chuckled, but Ji-Yeong didn't join in. His face remained serious.

"Did I hurt you?" Concern was etched across his handsome features.

"No. You didn't hurt me. Far from it." Tangling their fingers together, she wrapped his arm around her. "I'm just no longer used to that level of enthusiasm in the bedroom."

Maria didn't want to talk about her lack of a sex life since Oscar died, so she let her response trail off there. Bringing up one's dead husband tended to put a damper on amorous pursuits.

They relaxed there in silence with Maria appreciating being held and stroked by Ji-Yeong's strong hands. He had magic fingers capable of inspiring desire or comfort. It had been ages since she'd indulged in a soak in the bath. The fragrance of the essential oils was more than pleasing.

Ji-Yeong kissed the spot where her neck met her shoulder. While he was mostly clean-shaven, a hint of stubble tickled her skin causing her to shiver.

"Has the water gotten too cold?"

Before she could answer, he reached over to a console and pressed a button. Unseen jets released water. The increased heat felt wonderful.

"That feels amazing, but I was fine with the water temperature."

"Fine isn't good enough."

Ji-Yeong said it with such confidence her center clenched at the implications. She wondered what he did in his professional life, or life outside of Club Desire, which bolstered such self-assurance. She guessed it could be attributed, in some part, to his physical appearance. But, she'd known many attractive men who didn't have the presence Ji-Yeong wore around his neck like an Olympic gold medal.

When he began maneuvering her sideways on his lap, Maria didn't protest. Ji-Yeong's large palms glided along her thighs, his fingers curving into her flesh gently massaging the muscles. She didn't attempt to contain the moan his touch inspired.

Tucking her head beneath his chin, she leaned into him allowing him any access he desired. The caresses felt heavenly. Maria wouldn't dream of preventing his ministrations. He stroked her calves and even the bottoms of her feet before moving back up her leg, stopping just shy of her mons.

Without realizing it, she held her breath in anticipation of him dipping those talented fingers inside her again. Their time in the bath had a rejuvenating effect on her and she was ready for more of Ji-Yeong's lessons in pleasure.

Maria hadn't ever considered a younger man an option for her, but he was quickly changing her perspective on the matter. Although, it was possible he was an exception and not the standard.

When he didn't move his digits even a millimeter closer to her eager center, Maria began to squirm. She took some degree of pleasure when she noted the hardening of his shaft against her bum-bum. *Why had that phrase entered her mind at such a passion laden moment?* Either way, Maria was happy she wasn't the only one being denied.

"Beauty, do I have your permission to continue with the next round of our session?"

"God yes." Maria's agreement came immediately.

Ji-Yeong kissed along the column of her neck, but his fingers never moved any closer to her now pulsing core. Maria didn't understand. She'd given her permission why wasn't he doing something more than kissing her?

As if he read her thoughts, Ji-Yeong spoke directly into her ear.

"Remember, Beauty. I said you could have your way last time. This round, we do things my way. My way doesn't involve swift releases. I'm not a quick fuck, and neither are you."

Having made his declaration, he placed both hands on her hips, lifting her to stand before him. He immediately stood with her moving them away from the ledge they'd reclined on. Ji-Yeong's fingers wrapped around the back of her neck with his thumb beneath her jaw. Using it, he tipped her face up to accept his kiss.

Maria opened beneath his questing tongue as soon as he licked the seam of her lips. The moan in her throat never hit the air as he imprisoned it with his mouth, skillfully kissing her into following his lead without question. He trailed off into short pecks drawing a tiny grunt of irritation from her.

"Turn around. Put your hands on the bar."

Until he said something, Maria hadn't paid any attention to the high back side of the tub with a shiny chrome bar/railing running the length of it. It was slightly lower than waist-high. So, she had to lean forward to grasp it.

As soon as her fingertips connected with the warm metal, Ji-Yeong's hands were at her hips, encouraging her to tilt them higher. A palm between her shoulder blades gave silent instruction for her to lower her shoulders closer to the ledge. Due to the mirror along the back of the tub, she saw the appreciative way he stared at her body.

He looked at her like she was a buffet of all his favorite things to eat. Keeping with the theme her mind conjured, he dropped into a crouch behind her. With his hands lifting her ample bottom he pressed his face into her, unerringly latching onto her clit, sucking it into his mouth. He worried the sensitive bundle of nerves with his tongue. Maria's eyes slammed shut from the strong zing of pleasure shooting through her core.

The tug at her center was so strong, she was certain she was going to come even faster than she had the first time. It was good Ji-Yeong hadn't placed limitations on her vocalizing her enjoyment. Maria had transformed into a person she'd never met. A moaner, whose vocal appreciation was quickly escalating to keening wails. Just when she thought she was going to break apart from Ji-Yeong's skillful use of his tongue, he pulled away.

Her grunt of frustration was accompanied by a full-on pout. Maria's eyes popped open and she stared at him in disbelief as he stood tall behind her. The lines between her eyebrows disappeared when she saw the condom wrapper in his hand.

Maria's hips began an involuntary winding motion in anticipation. Ji-Yeong's hand landed on her ass, gripping, silently stilling her movements.

"Is your pussy eager for my dick, Beauty?"

Pressure at the opening of her channel made Maria's eyelids droop. Her mouth went dry as moisture gathered in the area most needed. Only, Ji-Yeong remained poised at her entrance without giving her the relief she sought. *What the hell was he waiting for?*

"Answer my question, Beauty. I can make Honey feel better than good, but you've gotta talk to me."

Maria replayed the last few minutes trying to remember what question he'd asked which really required a response. Her normally sharp mind was overcome with desire. Her only goal was fulfilling her lust. It took far longer than she wanted for the recent memory to resurface. He'd said something about her eager pussy and his dick. *Was that it?*

Ji-Yeong and his damn consent kink. It was obvious he had no intention of doing anything beyond teasing her until she admitted how much she wanted him.

"Yes damnit. I want your dick inside me."

Maria tried to rock her hips back to secure the prize she sought, but Ji-Yeong's hold on her cheeks prevented her from moving in any way he didn't want.

"What are you doing, Beauty? You get dick when I say. You come when I say. This isn't your boardroom. You don't have control tonight. I do."

Maria had never thought herself to be an impatient person, but she wanted to scream at the delay. However, his show of dominance also made her channel pulse in expectation of him delivering on every promise spoken. And unspoken.

"Do you understand me, Beauty?"

"Yes." It was soft, but clear. Maria had no memory of ever being denied something she wanted so desperately. *Was this what addiction felt like?* She was at the point where she'd do or say whatever Ji-Yeong demanded if it meant she'd get to experience the bliss of his cock stretching her walls again.

Chapter Ten

"Good girl."

Ji-Yeong crooned the words as he slid into her clasping velvet walls. He watched his length disappear between her puffy lips. Grateful for the stamina he'd developed over the years he was able to enjoy the erotic visual without blowing his load. Only after he was seated fully inside her heat did he break his stare to admire their reflection in the mirrored glass.

Maria's fingers squeezed the chrome rail tightly. Her lower lip was captured between her teeth. The action didn't mute her noises of pleasure. From the strained sound, he could tell she was still trying to maintain some arcane standard of control. *That wouldn't do.*

Ji-Yeong used his superior height to lean over her back to speak directly into her ear. While giving her shallow strokes, he encouraged her to let it go. He assured her she was safe to express herself completely with him. No one would hear.

"This is all for you, Beauty. My dick, my mouth, my fingers, my body are for your pleasure. You don't have to be ashamed to scream if you want."

Kissing her shoulders, then the back of her neck, he continued. "I have a confession. The more you mewl and moan, the harder it makes my dick, and the more I want to do the things to draw out those delicious sounds. Pleasing you pleases me, baby. So let me hear it."

On cue, Maria released a beautiful cross between a moan and a wail. Her head dropped to the side lying on her arm. Taking advantage of the length of neck exposed, Ji-Yeong rained kisses and nibbles along her skin.

He continued to drive her closer to orgasm. Teasing her nipples, he noticed the tightening of her channel when he pinched the beaded peaks. Continuing to offer praise for the trust she'd placed in him, he slid one hand over her belly seeking her pearl.

As soon as his fingers drew within an inch of the sensitive bundle of nerves, Maria's pussy started to flutter around his cock. She was too close. Reluctantly, he paused mid-stroke. Blind with lust, Maria rocked her hips back trying to keep the rhythm going.

Locking her in his embrace, Ji-Yeong put an end to her little excursion. His voice crackled with the growl he suppressed.

"Stop it. I'll let you know when it's time for *you* to fuck *me*."

Maria's movements stilled, but her chest heaved with each pant she released. Standing up straight, Ji-Yeong placed his hands on her hips to prevent her from following him, as he withdrew from her tempting pussy.

Ignoring her grumbling of protest, he coaxed her away from the railing and out of the tub. Snagging an oversized towel from the warming rack, he patted every inch of her body dry. Spending extra time on particular areas, he kept Maria's arousal hovering near the edge of release. But he never allowed her to tip over.

Once he was satisfied, he led her back into the bedroom. Leaving her lying on the bed, he went to the console. Grabbing the packet she'd fingered earlier, he dumped the contents into his hand before picking up the lightly scented lotion. When he turned back to Maria, he found her watching him beneath lust lowered lids.

Dangling the chain from one hand, he noticed the slight widening of her eyes. It wasn't fear. It was excitement. He'd made note of the way she'd handled the clamps earlier and had a hunch she'd warm up to the point where they could use them.

"What's your color?"

"Green."

Ji-Yeong's lips tipped into a smile as she writhed trying to relieve the pressure without actually touching her mons. He took pride in knowing she'd taken him at his word and had ceased trying to control her own plea-sure—at least for now.

Approaching the bed, he placed the lotion onto the bedside table. He perched on the edge beside Maria while he detangled the chain. Her gaze followed his movements, but she didn't say anything. Ji-Yeong watched the rise and fall of her chest along with the pulse at the base of her neck. He could tell that simply thinking about what he planned to do with the jewelry in his hands was turning her on.

"Do you remember this?" Ji-Yeong held up the silver links.

"Yes."

"What's your color?"

"Green."

"Do I have your permission to use these clamps on your nipples and clit, Beauty?"

"Will it hurt?"

Ji-Yeong shook his head. With one finger, he traced a circle around her areola. Her nipple hardened at the stimulation. Squeezing the turgid bud between his thumb and forefinger he explained.

"The sensation is similar to this, but with more focus." Holding one of the clamps closer to her face, he let her see it.

"There are no teeth on the clamps and there is a silicone coating easing the feel of them. We can tighten or loosen the hold to suit your comfort level."

He watched as Maria's thoughts played out across her face. Ji-Yeong guessed that her previously vanilla existence was at war with the vixen who was brave enough to walk into a sex club and spend the evening with a total stranger. Although, if he had anything to say about it, and he did, tonight wouldn't be their only foray into the indulgences of Club Desire.

"Yes. Let's do it."

"Are you certain?" As much as he wanted her to say yes, he also wanted an enthusiastic participant in all they did together.

"Yes. I want to try it."

Nodding, Ji-Yeong leaned over her capturing her lips. He'd allowed her ardor to cool a bit, but he didn't anticipate it would take much to get her back where he wanted her. His Beauty was so responsive, he had to remind himself they were in a scene. He couldn't get carried away. Not tonight.

Gathering both of her hands into one of his, he arranged them above her head. Pulling up the straps he'd requested, when he reserved the room, Ji-Yeong wrapped her fingers around them.

"Keep your hands here."

Maria's gaze was fixed on him. He detected the hint of rebellion lurking behind her eyes.

"Do you think you will be able to behave? Follow the rules? If not, I can fasten these around your wrists to help you."

Her dilated pupils told him she was aroused at the prospect of being strapped to the bed. He wouldn't do it though. Not yet. She probably thought she wanted it, but it would be too quick for their association. Bondage required more trust, and he wouldn't risk doing anything that stopped him from achieving his goal—making her come so hard and so often she forgot her own name.

Returning to her lips, Ji-Yeong kissed a path to her right breast. He sucked the pebbled peak between his teeth. Lashing it with his tongue, he prepared her for the clamp with his bite. Without warning, he replaced his teeth with the first clamp.

"MMM!!" Maria's response was immediate. Her legs twisted and she pressed her thighs together.

Not wasting time, Ji-Yeong performed the same routine on her left breast. Ji-Yeong traced the connecting chain dangling between her tits giving it a light tug. Her responding moan went straight to his cock. It was going to be fucking amazing when he was back inside her feeling her slick channel quivering around his shaft.

Using firm pressure, he encouraged her to open her legs. Lying on his stomach, he inhaled the tangy fragrance of her mons. He couldn't resist a quick lick. *Honey.* It's no wonder that's what he'd named her pussy. Her juices reminded him of honey. Just as sweet and twice as addictive.

Her bucking hips refocused him and he relocated his lips to the stiff little bundle of nerves peeking from its hood. Pressing both hands against her inner thighs, he regained control of her movements. Maria's pants and hoarse cries of desire sang out into the room egging him on.

Releasing her clit with a suckling pop, Ji-Yeong placed the last clamp.

Maria's gasp was immediate. When she didn't exhale quickly enough to suit him, he tapped her inner thigh with his palm.

"Breathe, Beauty."

Her breath released in a whoosh, causing her breasts to jiggle. The motion set off another gasp at the tugging of the clamps against the three sensitive areas of her body. He'd adjusted the length so that there was just enough slack to not be painful, but not enough to allow free movement without feeling the pull on at least one area.

"Fuck, Ji-Yeong..."

"What's your color?"

"Oh shit... I think... I think...Green."

"You think?" Ji-Yeong rested on his knees with her thighs thrown over his. Her eyes were barely visible beyond the slits left by her lashes, but he saw the lust present in their depths.

"Green." She moaned.

"Good girl."

Ji-Yeong plucked the lotion from the side table and began rubbing it all over Maria's body. Starting at her feet, he worked his way up. At random intervals, he paused in his massaging. He'd tug at the links joining the clamps to her nipples and clit. He'd kiss her peaks or lap at her folds. He paid no attention to the passage of time. His sole focus was on his Beauty.

He was rubbing the lotion onto her left hand, when he stopped and kissed her palm. Her fingers clenched around his and she released a tortured sigh.

"I can't, Ji-Yeong. Please, baby."

Releasing her fingers, he leaned over staring into her face. A sheen of wetness was gathered in her eyes. His fingers flexed to remove the clamps.

"What's your color?"

"Yellow."

Ji-Yeong nodded. He didn't let it show, but he internally cursed himself for not tracking her better. He didn't want her to teeter into pain.

"Does it hurt, Beauty? Do you want me to remove them?"

"No. It doesn't hurt. I just need to come. Please. Can I come?"

Ji-Yeong's cock was in full agreement with her request, but he wouldn't be rushed. Thankfully, for the both of them, he was done with her massage. Following the same order he'd used when he applied the clamps, he kissed each peak sucking the bud into his mouth as he removed it.

When the only clamp remaining was the one on her clit, he leaned back on his haunches. Notching his granite hard erection at the opening of her pussy, he slowly penetrated her walls. Maria's back arched and her head tipped backwards into the pillow. Her arms were taut as she tugged at the straps attached to the head board.

The visual was too much for him. Ji-Yeong couldn't prolong things any further. Unlatching the last clamp, he tossed the chain aside and rubbed her clit. Almost as soon as the pressure was released, Maria's cries reached a new octave and her channel trembled around his length with such strength it was impossible not to tumble with her into the abyss.

His hips jerked spasmodically as he emptied himself into the latex sheath. Ji-Yeong's labored breathing joined with Maria's as he wrapped his arms around her and rolled them to their sides while maintaining their connection. His cock jerked with after tremors in tandem with the grasping tugs of her pussy milking him.

There was no fucking way he was walking away from this woman after one night.

Chapter Eleven

Maria rolled over in the bed. The sunlight streaming into the room didn't inspire joy. Instead, she grumbled. She'd forgotten to pull the heavier curtains closed over the sheer drapes in front of the floor to ceiling windows of her hotel room. When she'd arrived from her night at Club Desire, she'd nearly fallen face first into the luxurious bedding. Closing the curtains hadn't been a thought in her mind.

Turning away from the brightness, she tugged the covers over her head. She wondered what time it was, but didn't have the motivation to even seek out a clock. Maria was content to lay there, but the outside world had other plans. The cellphone she'd placed on the nightstand began to vibrate, playing a DJ mix of hip-hop and rock. *Tahlia.*

Blindly searching the surface, Maria wrapped her fingers around the device. Pulling it beneath the covers with her, she tapped the screen.

"Tee...It's way too early in the morning."

"First of all, hello to you too. Secondly, It's damn near lunch time."

Maria whipped the covers off her head, held the phone away from her face and looked at the time on the display. *Shit!* Tahlia was right.

"Wow. I had no idea I'd slept so late."

"Mhmm. Sinister must have worked you over good if you're still in bed sleeping. You're welcome."

The reminder of the failed attempt had Maria pushing herself up to sit with her back against the headboard. Her lips twisted a little at the soreness of her muscles. Although, thanks to Ji-Yeong's attention to aftercare, she wasn't in a great deal of pain.

"I didn't thank you for that travesty, and I won't." Maria grumbled.

"What do you mean? When I didn't hear from you last night, I figured things were going well. After I didn't hear from you first thing this morning, I thought you must have gotten your back blown out for real."

"What I mean is the little shit showed up and immediately tried to put his hands on me thinking he could tell me what to do."

"The fuck?! You aren't serious."

"I wish I wasn't." Maria adjusted the covers and gave Tahlia the run down on her introduction and parting with Ian 'Sinister' George.

"M.E., I'm so sorry. He came highly recommended. You know me. I wanted you to knock off the cobwebs, but I wouldn't do that to you."

"So, you never played with him?"

"What?! Eww! We have boundaries remember? Of all the things we share, dick ain't one of them."

Maria placed the call on speaker, leaving her hands free to pluck at the comforter thrown across her lap. "I didn't know if those rules applied in a place like Club Desire. It's not like people are in there making love matches."

Even as she spoke the words to her friend, Maria felt a ping she refused to acknowledge as jealousy. Thinking of Ji-Yeong doing to anyone else what he'd done to her didn't sit right with her. Realistically, she knew it made no sense. They'd shared a few...well...more like six passionate hours. Their time together in no way meant either of them had a claim on the other.

"For your information, many a love match has been made in Club Desire. But, since I signed the same NDA you did, that's as much as I can say about it."

Maria wasn't interested in who Tahlia referenced, but she was intrigued at the thought of people making lasting connections with someone they'd met under those circumstances.

"So, if you didn't have a session with Sinister, why are you still in bed?

It's not like you need to recuperate from having your under-used lady bits put to work."

A wry grin tilted Maria's lips. "Ma'am, you really shouldn't make assumptions. I told you Sinister was escorted out. I never said I left behind him."

A few beats of silence hung between them. Maria waiting for her unspoken message to sink in with Tahlia. Tahlia was apparently waiting on Maria to give up more details.

"Noooo..." Maria wasn't sure how she should feel about the disbelief in her friend's voice.

"What? I was already there. Just because the guy I was supposed to meet turned out to be an asshole dud, didn't mean my night had to be over."

"M.E.! What did you do?"

Maria giggled at Tahlia's shocked accusation. "A sexy Asian man who had a very interesting specialty."

"Shut! Up!" Tahlia reverted to her teenaged self. When Maria literally went quiet, her friend screeched.

"Trick! Don't you clam up on me. I need deets! That's a huge step for you."

"Non-Disclosure Agreement remember?"

"Fuck a NDA. You don't have to give me his name, you can call him Sam for all I care. I want to know if you got your pipes cleaned and your guts rearranged."

Maria shook her head, giggling at Tahlia's antics. She couldn't help torturing her a little longer.

"Since when do we give blow by blows of sexual conquests?"

"Since I dropped $250k to get you into an exclusive sex club."

Maria put her hand over her face laughing at Tahlia. She knew her friend was serious.

"Please, we both know the fee didn't hurt your pockets and you'll find a way to write it off on your taxes."

"Of course I will, but I'll use whatever tools available to me to get you to tell me why your voice did that thing when you just mentioned Sam's existence."

"Sam?"

"You said you hooked up with a Sexy Asian Man. So... Sam. You know. To keep his anonymity, and keep you on the right side of the NDA"

Maria couldn't fault her logic, although she found Tahlia's way of saying it amusing. They'd been best friends since their mid-thirties. At the time, they were both married. Now, Tahlia was divorced and Maria was a widow.

She knew her friend was wildin' for a few years after her divorce, but they'd never given blow by blows of sexual exploits. Simply knowing the other's needs were being handled was enough. So, Tahlia's demand was new. As she was deciding how much or little to reveal to her friend, her phone buzzed with an incoming text message.

> Ji-Yeong Kang: Good Afternoon, Beauty. How are you feeling?

Maria froze. Her pulse thudded as vivid memories of the last time she saw Ji-Yeong flooded her mind. She recalled his tenderness as he sat with her in his lap on the bench in the shower. He simply cradled her in his arms after cleansing her body. They left the room with her tucked into his side, and he waited with her until her hired car came to pick her up. Maria didn't recall them exchanging numbers, but there was his name, big and bold, on her cellphone display.

"M.E.!"

"Huh?" Maria was snatched out of her memories by Tahlia's voice.

"Where did you go? Did something happen?"

It didn't cross Maria's mind to play it off. "Um... He just texted me."

"Which, He? Sam, He?"

"Yes."

"Y'all exchanged numbers? Girl, that sounds like more than a one-time hook up."

"I honestly don't remember doing it, but his name is right here on my screen and he just messaged me. So, it's a good bet that it happened." Maria gnawed on her bottom lip.

"What do I do, Tee?" It had been exactly twenty-six years since she'd been at this stage with any man.

"It depends. Did you have a good time with him?"

"Yes."

"You obviously felt safe enough to give him your number. So, would you be interested in seeing him again?"

Maria's immediate thought was absolutely. But, it wasn't a question of if she wanted to see him, it was a matter of *should she*.

"I don't know if it's a good idea for me to see him again."

"Why not?"

"Being with a guy just for sex isn't my baseline. I think it might be better for me to end things here before I get attached."

"Damn...He knocked those cobwebs off good didn't he?"

Maria frowned. Tahlia wasn't taking her concerns seriously. Maria allowed her silence to speak for her.

"Come on, M.E. We both know sex doesn't have to equal a relationship. So, tell me what's really bothering you."

Maria recaptured her bottom lip. Her response was more of a mumble.

"Excuse me? I didn't understand you." Tahlia was goading her, but Maria fell into the trap anyway.

"I said, he's significantly younger than me."

"How young? Like Jared young?"

Maria shivered at the suggestion of doing what she'd done with Ji-Yeong with someone her twenty-year old son's age.

"No! Of course not."

"Then what do you consider significantly younger?"

"At least ten years."

"Wait. You don't know for sure?"

"I didn't exactly ask. I estimated based on how he looked. He had slight sprinkles of barely noticeable gray, but his skin was smooth. No wrinkles or even frown lines."

"Girl, bye. That doesn't mean anything. You damn near have to show ID for people to believe you're over thirty-five. For all you know the man's genes could be blessing him with a youthful appearance."

"I don't think so."

"Anyway, it doesn't matter. He's not a child. He's an adult. An adult who is obviously interested in remaining connected to you. It's up to you to decide if you want to continue."

"I don't know."

"M.E., it's not like the man is proposing marriage. He could be a nice distraction while you're in the Windy City. You have a few days left there before you head home. Why not let Sam keep blowing out your back? That way, you don't have to break in anyone new."

Maria's fingers hovered above the phone as she considered her friend's advice. Finally, she tapped out a response.

Chapter Twelve

Ji-Yeong had managed to hold off until after noon before contacting Maria. It wasn't a desire to appear cool and unfazed which kept him from reaching out. It was the knowledge that she'd need at least five hours of rest.

The sun was peeking over the horizon when he'd made it to his condo after seeing Maria off from the club. If it had taken her roughly the same amount of time to reach her hotel, it was almost six in the morning before she made it to bed. The two of them hadn't slept during their time together.

They played for a couple of hours more before he called a halt to things and began aftercare. During that time, they talked. He creatively tried to find out as much as he could about her. Once they were dressed, he secured her phone number. He called her to make sure she locked his in as well.

He wasn't happy to put her into a hired car, but when he saw the plates on the limo, he recognized it as a reputable company. Still, as soon as he was sure she'd gotten some rest, he was tapping away at his phone trying to connect with his Beauty.

Once he'd sent the message, Ji-Yeong found himself watching the phone in his hand, waiting for a response. Realizing what he was doing, he placed it on the ottoman and sat back on the sofa. He couldn't obsess about this. If she responded, great. If she didn't, that was fine too.

The quietness of the room was entirely too loud. Ji-Yeong's gaze swept around looking for the remote control. Flipping his wrist, he checked the time. Maybe there was a game about to start. Chicago had all the major sports covered. So, there was bound to be an event to capture his attention.

Ji-Yeong jumped and scrambled toward his phone when the message alert rang out. It was a good thing there was no one around to witness his lack of suaveness when he snatched up the device.

> Beauty: I'm okay.

Ji-Yeong's response was immediate. Fuck playing it cool. Besides, he genuinely cared how she was feeling. He knew he'd pushed some physical limits during their time together. He blamed it on the uncertainty he'd have another chance—despite knowing he'd use every resource available to him to make sure he saw her again.

> Ji-Yeong: Are you really? We had quite a workout last night.

> Beauty: My thighs are a little sore, but it's to be expected.

A sly grin took over Ji-Yeong's face as he recalled the ways he'd maneuvered her body into various positions while they played. The memory of her thick thighs stretched wide to accommodate him had his length hardening in his jeans.

> Ji-Yeong: Texting isn't my thing. I'm going to call you.

He'd barely hit send on the message before he tapped the icon to place the call. Once it was connected, Ji-Yeong unconsciously held his breath waiting to hear her voice. When she spoke, he detected the scratchiness from when they'd parted ways earlier that morning.

"Hello, Ji-Yeong."

"Good afternoon, Beauty. Would you like a massage? I could arrange it for you."

Maria's throaty chuckle went straight to his cock. *Down boy.*

"You're sweet to offer, but your massages are what got me into this situation to begin with."

"I would say, I'm sorry..."

"But you're not, and neither am I. Besides, I don't want an apology."

"What do you want, then?" Ji-Yeong leaned back on the couch, propping his feet on the ottoman. Before she answered, he heard an unmistakable sound.

"You don't have to tell me. Your stomach just did."

"Oh my God! I can't believe that just happened."

Suppressing his laughter, Ji-Yeong reassured her. "It's not a big deal. I'm guessing you haven't eaten yet today."

"No. Honestly I've been awake for less than an hour. I guess I was wiped out."

"Well, you did expend a lot of energy last night and earlier this morning. If you weren't at least a little tired, I'd think I failed at my mission."

Ji-Yeong heard rustling which he associated with bed coverings and shut his eyes. He called up the memory of her lying next to him curled into his side after their final round of play in the wee hours. The stiffness in his pants was becoming uncomfortable.

Clearing his throat, Ji-Yeong attempted to direct his thoughts away from sexual things. At least for the moment. By the end of their thirty-minute conversation, he'd secured her agreement to spend the day with him. He'd conceded to meeting her at the restaurant in her hotel, but he wouldn't budge on planning the rest of their activities.

He'd learned during their cuddle session that she was in Chicago for the next three days, and she'd only visited the city once before. The condo was one of his seven properties he considered home as he moved between continents being a digital nomad. He was typically in the city at some point during the Spring and Fall. It was rare for him to brave a blustery winter there. Not when he could be sitting on the beach at his villa in Bali.

The beauty of having various properties in desirable places was he could list them on luxury vacation rental sights during times when he wasn't using them. He kept staff on hand at each place to maintain them. So, they were always ready for potential guests. He'd recently rented his villa to Carver Jamison. The professional football coach wanted a secure location to have his wedding and had been willing to pay Ji-Yeong's list price plus extra for the additional staff.

The pictures of Carver and his beautiful wife, Alyssa, were plastered all over social media for weeks following the event. He and Carver were close enough acquaintances that Ji-Yeong had his staff remove his personal belongings from the master suites and opened them up for their use. Since his properties tended to have large accommodations, certain rooms and spaces were designated as off limits.

Ji-Yeong arrived at the hotel restaurant only minutes before Maria. He didn't disguise his hunger for her as he watched her approach. Even dressed casually in fitted jeans, a peach top and comfortable flats, she captured all his attention. Her hair was, once again, pinned up off her neck. He couldn't wait to muss it up.

Greeting her with a light kiss on the cheek they entered the restaurant. Ji-Yeong enjoyed watching as her demeanor vacillated between, what he'd gathered, was her normal self-confident persona and a slightly shy woman. The shy woman avoided direct eye contact at times, but the self-confident Beauty met his banter with her own snazzy comebacks.

Once they were done with their meals, it was time to take her on the tour she'd failed to have during her previous visit. It included a trip to the giant silver bean downtown. Then, he purchased her a few bags of the famous popcorn before they headed to Lake Shore Drive, continuing on to a nearby park and beach. It was very touristy, but Maria appeared to enjoy it.

As the sun began to set, they entered the parking garage attached to his condo building. Ji-Yeong was mildly surprised it hadn't taken much convincing to get her to agree to dinner at his place. He'd jokingly referenced the massage he'd promised her earlier only to have her give him side eye. The increase in her pulse belied her attempt to appear nonchalant.

Maria's eyes swept around the space when they entered his condo. Ji-Yeong wondered what she saw when she looked at the cream-colored furnishings and muted shades throughout. The only pops of color were in the paintings on the wall. Of which there were only two.

Considering her perspective made Ji-Yeong realize the place looked like corporate housing rather than someone's home—even if he only lived there, on average, a few months out of the year. Instead of dwelling on his interior design choices, he focused his attention on the beautiful woman beside him.

Offering her a pair of slippers, Ji-Yeong removed his shoes placing them on a rack near the door. Maria accepted the slippers and followed suit.

"This is a nice place. Even from way over here, I can tell the view is amazing." She tilted her head toward the large picture windows making up almost an entire wall of the living room.

"Thank you. Feel free to have a closer look."

Ji-Yeong agreed with her about the view. It was one of the reasons he'd chosen to keep this unit for himself when he purchased the building. He couldn't keep his eyes off Maria as she walked to the windows. The way she moved enchanted him. Her confidence, her grace tempered by a hint of innocence which seemed improbable for someone with as much life experience as she had.

During lunch, she'd broached the subject of their age difference. He was surprised to learn she was fifteen years older than him, but it didn't matter. Nothing short of her saying she didn't want him would dissuade him from pursuing her. Even then, he might not believe her. A body doesn't respond the way hers did for someone she didn't want. He'd just have to work on turning her lust into something more.

Chapter Thirteen

Maria gazed out at the city. What Ji-Yeong referred to as his condo was actually a penthouse apartment in a building she was certain had units priced in the seven-figure range. The view from the floor-to-ceiling windows was breathtaking. The sun set over the city painting the sky in orange bleeding into red and violet.

So far, they'd had a really nice day. Her pulse thudded in a steady rhythm as she considered what might happen next. She wasn't under the illusion they'd come back to his place to simply share a meal and talk. He had promised her a massage, and they both knew where that could lead.

It wasn't guaranteed her body could handle another marathon with Ji-Yeong. But Tahlia was right. Maria should make the most out of her weekend. Coming across another person so well versed in pleasing her was like playing the lottery. It was highly improbable. She'd already won an all-expense paid trip to orgasm land. Why should she walk away without enjoying the full experience?

Warmth enveloped her as Ji-Yeong wrapped her in his arms. His lips grazed the crook of her neck before kissing behind her ear.

"I ordered dinner. It should be here shortly."

"Thank you. You didn't have to do that."

"Of course I did, Beauty. Nourishment is important."

Maria squelched the shiver skating down her spine from the baritone of his voice tickling her ears calling her *Beauty*. There was no guile in his mention of providing nourishment. He planned to do filthy things to her. She knew it. She *welcomed* it.

"If you say so, Mr. Kang."

Ji-Yeong's arms tightened around her. Maria gasped when he nipped her lobe with his teeth. She wore platinum stud earrings, so there was very little deterrent to his pursuit.

"Have I told you how sexy it is hearing you call me that?"

"Really, Mr. Kang? I had no idea."

Maria grinned, but didn't take her gaze off the Chicago skyline lighting up in the darkening sky. Ji-Yeong wasn't the only observant one. She'd caught the way his lashes lowered slightly and his square jaw ticked when she'd called him Mr. Kang during lunch. At the time, Maria had simply filed the knowledge away for future use. It was nice to know she could also wield words affecting him the way him calling her *Beauty* affected her.

"Beauty...You are playing a dangerous game. You're talking like a woman who wants to be eaten instead being fed."

Finally taking her eyes off the buildings outside the window, Maria turned in his embrace. Lifting on her tip toes, she slid her arms up his chest resting her hands at the nape of his neck. His silky hair tickled her fingertips.

"Why can't I have both?"

"Woman..." Ji-Yeong growled in warning. She lifted a challenging eyebrow.

"Ooo!" Maria squeaked when he grabbed the backs of her thighs and lifted her against him. Her legs automatically tightened around his waist.

Ji-Yeong strode through the room into a short hallway and another door before depositing her on a large platform bed. The plush bedcoverings gave way beneath her cocooning Maria in softness. She had no time to acclimate to her new position prior to his hands skimming her waist, unbuttoning her pants.

His face was a mask of intensity and focus, making her insides quiver in anticipation. The man had already proven, multiple times, that he was gifted in the area of dispensing pleasure. Air had barely hit her legs before he tossed them over his shoulders and dove face first into her pussy. There was really no other way to describe the way he approached the task.

Simply based on the sounds he made as he lapped at her folds and delved into her center, it was obvious he enjoyed giving as much as she enjoyed receiving. When he sucked her clit between his lips and lashed it with his tongue, Maria's brain shut down anything unrelated to appreciating the pleasure Ji-Yeong provided.

"Ah Shit! Oh Fuck!"

Maria cried out as she fell over the precipice into an orgasm. *Damn*. It hadn't even taken him a solid five minutes to get her there. She swore she heard Ji-Yeong growl as he consumed the offering her body released. Her legs shook, and he licked her sweet spot through the tremors of her orgasm.

When she finally stopped shaking, he placed parting kisses on her mons and her inner thighs. Resting on his elbows between her spread legs, he looked up at her. Beneath half lowered eyelids, she returned his stare.

"We need to work on your O-control."

"Mmm...I thought your whole deal was making sure I didn't try to control things?"

Standing from where he knelt on the floor, Ji-Yeong climbed onto the bed, removing the remainder of her clothing along the way.

"There's a difference between not allowing yourself to become fully immersed in the moment and training your body to hold off on climaxing."

Ji-Yeong rained kisses on her body as he exposed more skin. His nimble fingers flicked open her bra releasing her breasts. Her nipples pebbled. Maria honestly didn't know if it was from the cool air or the hungry expression on Ji-Yeong's face as he looked at them. The way he worshipped her body made everything she'd seen as an imperfection disappear. The evidence of her carrying her son became a badge of honor as he kissed her stomach and cupped her breasts in his large hands.

Just as he took one turgid peak between his lips, a melodic tone joined their heaving breaths. Ji-Yeong's reluctance to let go of his treat was obvious. Maria was #TeamIgnoreIt, but he was already on the move.

"That's our dinner. Don't move. I'll be right back."

They weren't in a scene, but his directive glued Maria to the mattress.

When he returned to the room, she remained exactly as he'd left her—legs bent at the knee and hanging over the side of the bed.

Silently, she watched as he stripped off his clothing. Although she'd seen the view last night, it was still a spectacular showing. He was large, but his body was lean with more a swimmer's build. When Ji-Yeong removed his boxer briefs, Maria's core clenched at the appearance of his beautiful cock.

Beautiful and cock were not two words she'd normally link together, but his was the exception. Long, with ample girth, and prominent veins traversing the length, his dick made her mouth water to taste him. During their session the previous night, he'd been clear in his mission to please her. So, she didn't get a chance to reciprocate.

Maria rose to a seated position on the bed, determined to satisfy her curiosity in all ways when it came to Ji-Yeong. She had to know what he looked like when he reached his peak while receiving oral. Once he was within reach, she wrapped her fingers around his shaft. She watched in awe as it thickened in her hands.

"Do you have something you wanna say, Beauty? Or is this all show and no tell?"

One corner of Maria's lips tipped up. Not bothering to meet his gaze or verbalize a response, she leaned forward swiping her tongue along the slit of his cockhead. A bit of precum appeared and she eagerly licked it away. Then, she flattened her tongue and took as much of his length, as she could manage, into her mouth. What she couldn't fit, she used her hand to stimulate

"Okay... Showing is good."

Ji-Yeong's voice was strained taking some of the edge off the sarcasm. His hands found their way to her head. He didn't push or try to guide her. It felt as if he simply had to touch her in some way. His digits released the pins and clamps she'd used to keep her thick curls contained. Maria moaned when his fingertips began massaging her scalp. Her moan was followed by a tortured groan from Ji-Yeong.

"Damn..." The single word appeared to be all he could manage.

It sent a tingle of pride through Maria for her efforts to render a man like Ji-Yeong speechless. Bobbing on his thickness, she used her free hand to cup his balls, carefully kneading the sac to heighten his pleasure. The combination of her attention to the sensitive area, and the way she took his cock to the back of her throat must have been Ji-Yeong's undoing.

"Fuck, Beauty."

The words were growled seconds before he tugged his cock away and lifted her fully onto the bed. Following her down, he notched his shaft at her opening and began steadily feeding his length into her channel. Maria gasped at the sensation of being filled. The way he stretched her walls rode the edge between pleasure and pain which was in the arena of absolute bliss.

Her hands roamed over his hard body marveling at the way he used it to drive her desire higher and higher. She lifted her legs to cradle his hips as he worked them in an amazing, breath-stealing rhythm.

When she inhaled deeply without releasing the breath, Ji-Yeong was in her ear coaching her to breathe. When she began gasping like she was on the verge of cumming, he was in her ear again commanding her to hold on. Telling her it wasn't time yet.

Maria's body responded to Ji-Yeong's demands in ways it had never listened to her. He rose to his knees and lifted her leg to his shoulder. There wasn't an ounce of protest from her previously sore muscles, when he leaned forward pressing her knee toward her armpit.

Instead, her body accommodated the new position and her pussy gushed. The position gave him the perfect angle for his cock to stimulate that special place inside her on every stroke.

"Now, Beauty. Now you can come all over my cock."

Maria didn't need further encouragement. Her keening wails were the backdrop to her quivering release. Ji-Yeong's sounds of pleasure joined with hers as his hips pumped until his pelvis was pressed so tightly against hers, air couldn't find its way between them. As Maria came down, she stared into Ji-Yeong's eyes as his cock jerked, releasing his hot cum inside her.

Chapter Fourteen

Ji-Yeong saw the look on Maria's face when she realized what had just happened between them. It was out of character for him, but he couldn't bring himself to regret it. He hadn't gone bare with anyone since his divorce more than a decade ago. Although she'd hinted she was beyond the age for more children, it wouldn't have been a concern because he'd undergone a vasectomy years ago.

Unlike some men, he followed the doctor's instructions and went to every follow up appointment to be certain the surgery remained successful. The feel of her velvet walls wrapped around his dick with nothing between them was instantly addictive. But...he still should have asked her if it was okay.

Lifting his weight from her, he slowly withdrew from his new favorite place and sat back on his knees. His eyes were magnetically drawn to her puffy lower lips. Despite having just blown his load, his cock twitched with the first pearlescent drop that appeared before it dripped downward. The sight made him want to bury himself inside her and start the process all over again.

Instead, he extended his hand and used his finger to catch the essence, rubbing it on the outside of her pussy like a moisturizer. Maria's hiss was immediately followed by a moan. Hearing her pleasure spurred him to continue his erotic stimulation.

Seeking her pearl, he added the sensitive nub into the rotation. As much as he wanted to plunge back inside her, he didn't. Ji-Yeong rubbed her clit until his Beauty reached another, softer orgasm. She shook lightly with after tremors. Giving a quick kiss to her lips, above and below, Ji-Yeong left the bed.

Once he had the bathroom prepared, he returned scooping the uber-relaxed Maria into his arms. She didn't utter a word. She simply tucked her head beneath his chin and snuggled into his chest. Stopping to cover her hair, Ji-Yeong walked into the shower. Immediately sitting on the bench built out from the back wall, he arranged her on his lap.

"How are you feeling?"

He nuzzled the side of Maria's neck and rubbed his hands along her back and over her thighs.

"Mmm...I feel good."

"Just good? It sounds like I need to try harder."

"If you try any harder, I'll need new hips and a new body to keep up."

They shared a soft laugh as the water pelted the tiles and filled the space with steam. Eventually, Ji-Yeong lifted the detachable shower head from its base and began to cleanse Maria's body. He wasn't sure how he felt about the twinge of regret he experienced when he washed away the last of his cum. It was new, but everything about the past two days was what he wanted in his life.

As physically beautiful as he found Maria, and as dynamic as they were together sexually, he admired other things about her. Her intelligence, her strength, her resilience and sense of self were just as sexy as her willingness to follow his lead in a scene.

Once they were showered and redressed—him in athletic shorts and a T-shirt and her in his spare robe—they were seated at his dining room table. The food was delicious, but it didn't hold a candle to Maria and her sweet bounty. Thinking of her sweetness brought him to the topic he knew he needed to address. Laying his fork down, he captured her attention.

"I owe you an apology, Beauty."

Maria mimicked his actions, placing her fork on her partially full plate. She didn't ask why he was apologizing, she simply watched and waited.

"I told you last night that everything we did together would be consensual."

"It has been."

"Not entirely. I failed to get your permission today when I came inside you bare. It's not like me. I apologize."

Maria searched his eyes, but he wasn't certain what she was looking for. After a few beats, she picked up her fork again.

"I accept your apology. You're right. We should've discussed it before we took that step." She speared a piece of chicken covered in Alfredo sauce onto the tines.

"But, I don't regret it. It was..." Her eyes darkened as her sentence trailed off.

"Fucking amazing." Ji-Yeong supplied.

"Yeah. That." Maria smiled and dug into her meal.

With the topic out in the open, they slipped into the unsexy, but necessary, conversation about medical history. They both received test and check-up results electronically via a secure medical app. So, they were able to share those with one another. Although, Ji-Yeong's gut told him it wasn't necessary. Maria wasn't the kind of woman who'd lie about whether she carried a harmful disease or infection.

An hour later, they were cuddled on the couch. Ji-Yeong's legs were stretched out in front of him on the ottoman and Maria was tucked into his side. They were supposed to be watching a movie. Instead, they were both teasing one another heading directly down the path of the *chill* portion of the evening.

The action on the screen was soon forgotten as the action on the sofa heated up. Ji-Yeong discovered, the more he and Maria came together, the more uninhibited she became. It made her even more appealing to him. And, considering how irresistible he found her, that was a high bar.

When she tugged at the waistband of his shorts to release his cock and slid down his length, Ji-Yeong was in heaven. With both hands filled with her voluptuous ass, he immersed himself in enjoying his Beauty unfettered. There was absolutely, zero fucking chance he was going to let this woman get away from him.

~

Ji-Yeong hugged Maria to his chest. Dropping his head, he inhaled her scent. They stood just inside the door of her hotel room. He'd been trying to leave her there and go back to his place for the past twenty minutes. It was understandable for him to have difficulty, since he hadn't wanted to bring her back there to begin with.

But, she needed a change of clothes and he'd agreed to give her a little space. They would only be separated for half the day, but Ji-Yeong couldn't seem to make his arms let go nor his feet move toward the door. Maria wasn't making it any better by rubbing his back and nuzzling the space between his pecs.

"If I didn't know you'd made a commitment and you like to keep your word, I would encourage us trying out that big ass bed over there. I've only slept on it a few hours, but I think it could serve our purposes just fine."

"Don't tempt me." Ji-Yeong groaned as he held her tighter.

If he hadn't set up this meeting weeks ago, he would've canceled and taken Maria up on her offer. Hell. Who was he kidding? He would've bought her new clothes and kept her at his place. She wouldn't have seen the inside of this hotel room again until she was ready to get her things to fly home.

Finally, he released her. Pressing a quick kiss to her lips, he stepped back. With his hand on the door handle, he looked at her.

"I'll see you later, Beauty."

"Later."

There was something in Maria's eyes which almost made him say, fuck it. But, Ji-Yeong managed to open the door to leave. Reminding her to put on the safety latch, he stepped into the hall. He didn't move until he heard the sound he was waiting for, letting him know she'd followed his instructions.

He made it back to his place in time to change into a button-down shirt and get settled behind his computer in his office. Ji-Yeong and a few other investors were looking into starting a new venture. This had been the only day, and time, the entire group was available to meet. They spent the next two hours going over the prospectus before resolving to think on it individually and come back together in a few days.

Once the conference call ended, Ji-Yeong picked up his cellphone. He had more plans to make. After only two rings, Elijah's voice floated over the line. Ji-Yeong was surprised he was the one who answered. He'd expected the daytime receptionist, not the owner of Club Desire.

Since he had him in person, Ji-Yeong followed up with Elijah about what happened with Sinister. Of course, he'd left Elijah a message about it the very next day. Elijah confirmed he'd already heard about it through Bethany and his security manager.

He assured Ji-Yeong the poor excuse for a Dom was banned from the club. Elijah had also put the word out to a few of his friends who owned similar establishments to be aware of Sinister's methods.

"I'm sure you didn't call to talk to me about tuning up some prick at the club, Gee. So, what can I do for you?"

"I actually didn't expect to speak to you at all today. I planned to follow up with you later in the week. I called to make some arrangements for my room tonight. Is the concierge around?"

"She stepped away. So, you got me instead. Bethany is here though. I'm sure she can help get the ball rolling."

"Thanks, Elijah. Good talking to you."

"Same. Hold on, I'll send you over to Bethany."

Ji-Yeong turned his wrist to check the time. It was still relatively early in the day. When the heck did Bethany go home and sleep?

Chapter Fifteen

Maria peeked at Ji-Yeong from the corner of her eye. He sat beside her silently with her hand clasped in his. Other than telling her they were going to the club, he hadn't given her any clues to the evening he planned. They'd just left the restaurant which had an excellent view of Lake Michigan in the fading daylight.

The meal was delicious, and the conversation was light. Although, Maria sensed a bit of heaviness weighing over them. It was her last night in Chicago before she boarded her flight back to Georgia and her life there. The past few days had far exceeded her expectations.

When she first walked through the doors of Club Desire, she'd had no idea she'd encounter a man like Ji-Yeong. A man who broke down her barriers and took her to unimaginable heights of pleasure. If she were honest with herself, she didn't want it to end.

But...she had a life to return to in Logan City. People had placed a great deal of trust in her to lead Fortitude into the future. It wasn't just her career. She also had Jared. He may not need her to be a hands-on mom. However, that didn't mean he didn't need her at all.

The vehicle came to a stop in front of the now familiar brick building. Ji-Yeong stepped out and reached inside to help Maria. As they approached the doors of the club, Maria marveled once again at how unassuming the building looked in comparison to the decadent hedonism which occurred behind those tinted windows and black door.

This time, when she entered the club, Bethany greeted her by her first name. There was no need for additional paperwork as the blonde waved to her and Ji-Yeong. They bypassed the downstairs lounge and headed straight for the elevator. Once they were inside, his fingers hovered over the buttons.

"Would you like to stop on the second floor?"

The fire in his eyes telegraphed his arousal. She could almost see the thought playing across his mind of pleasuring her while she watched another erotic scene play out on the dais. The mental image induced a flutter in her core. How far she'd come in less than seventy-two hours was amazing.

Placing her hand over his, she moved his finger to the button for the third floor. They had enough heat between them to get things going without watching other people to warm up. Besides, she didn't want to share him, not even visually, with anyone else tonight.

Nodding in understanding, he selected the third floor. They silently watched the indicator change as the car swiftly moved between the levels. The energy in the space was palpable. When the doors slid open they wasted no time exiting.

Maria had no idea what to expect when they reached the room Ji-Yeong reserved. Considering what he'd managed to do without foreknowledge on their first night together, her mind whirled with the possibilities. With the wealth of things he knew about her now, it was assured she'd have an experience to reflect on for years to come.

She tried not to let the temporariness of their time sadden her. This weekend would live on her life highlight reel. Maria would have to work hard to give Tahlia a comparable, just-because, gift sometime in the near future.

When Ji-Yeong opened the door, she stepped into a completely new dimension. Although the label on the door designated it as the room they'd used before, only the furniture was somewhat similar. Even those had been enhanced. The space had been transformed into an erotic fairy fantasy. Shrouded in sensual low lights, it sang *Sexy* like an operatic aria by a premier Diva.

Twinkling lights had been laced through the gossamer fabric attached to the canopy over the bed. Votive style candles were strategically placed around the room. It wasn't until she walked near one that Maria realized they were LED candles. They flickered so realistically, she'd thought they were traditional wax candles.

Stopping when she reached the center of the room, Maria turned to look at Ji-Yeong. He remained next to the door leaning against it. Desire coated his expression. Yet he made no attempt to come any closer. Wondering if he felt the same weight of their impending separation, Maria approached him.

He met her halfway. Folding her into his embrace, he lowered his head nuzzling the side of her face. His breathing was heavy in her ear sending a shiver down her spine. Cupping the side of his face, she locked eyes with him.

"Is everything okay?"

"That depends."

"On what?" Maria's pulse picked up as she studied his serious countenance.

"On if you will continue to treat this like it will be the last time we ever see each other."

Maria flinched slightly at the accuracy of his accusation. He'd gone directly to the heart of the matter without a hint of guile. She wanted to deny the truth of it, but she couldn't.

"Isn't it? I go home tomorrow and you go wherever place is next on your list. We live two very different lifestyles, Ji-Yeong."

"Actually, we don't. And I won't let you use our different career paths as an excuse to avoid even the possibility of there being an *us*."

Maria stared at him. She could barely hear herself think for the pounding of her heart. As illogical as it sounded, she'd fallen for Ji-Yeong Kang. Almost from the moment he lowered his frame onto the seat at the bar, three nights ago, and turned his chocolate eyes in her direction. But she came to Club Desire for an experience. She had no intention of finding love. Besides, could a relationship flourish after starting under the haze of desire? After twenty years of marriage, she knew it took more than good sex to sustain a life together.

"Ji-Yeong..."

"No, Maria. Don't do that. Don't resurrect your barriers because you want to control every aspect of your life, hoping it will mean you don't have to worry about falling in love again and possibly losing that person as well."

Maria stiffened. She tried to remove herself from his arms, but Ji-Yeong wouldn't allow it. She didn't want to face the truth of his words while feeling the warmth of his embrace.

"Let me go please."

"No."

Her eyes flew to his face at his immediate denial. Maria's brow furrowed. She squinted at him.

"I thought you said everything we did together would be consensual?"

"Don't use my words to avoid dealing with your feelings, Maria."

"Stop calling me Maria!"

"What else should I call you? Elena? Ms Stokes?"

Maria pursed her lips, staring at him mutinously. He knew damn well what she meant. He'd only referred to her by her given name the night they met. Even then, it was only for a brief time. She'd been his *Beauty* for the past three days and he had the audacity to switch things up on her now.

"Talk to me. What shall I call you other than your name?" When she didn't answer, he moved one hand to wrap around the back of her neck. His thumb stroked along her jaw as he tilted her head up towards his.

"I have suggestions, but they involve your acceptance of a few changes."

Ji-Yeong's lips ghosted over her forehead, then her nose before lightly grazing her lips. Maria lowered her lashes trying not to get caught up in his sensual haze. It was a lost cause, but she made an attempt.

The arm banded around her shifted and she felt Ji-Yeong's other large hand cupping her ass. When he squeezed the plump cheek, heat ignited in her center. He knew she adored how his hands felt on her.

"Do you want to hear my suggestions?"

Ji-Yeong rained kisses along Maria's neck and across her collarbone. The halter style dress she wore gave him easy access to the area. Maria's resolve was fading fast. *Why was she fighting this again?*

She knew what he wanted. The question hanging between them was, did she have the courage to relinquish control and take a chance? Her days were routine. Familiar. She'd finally adjusted to life alone. Was she ready to try adding someone else to her new normal? What would it look like with someone who had just as many, if not more responsibilities than she had?

Plunging her thoughts into the carnal realm and away from the logistics of combining lives, Ji-Yeong slipped his fingers into the bodice of her dress. She'd paid a pretty penny for the strapless number to hold up her generous breasts without a bra. So, he immediately met skin and captured a nipple between his thumb and forefinger. Maria's moan was accompanied by a clenching of her muscles as if her pussy was already milking him of his seed.

"Answer my question." Ji-Yeong increased the pressure on her taut bud. "Do you want to hear my suggestions?"

"Mmm...Yes." Maria was entering the *say anything* phase of the discussion. Whatever it took to achieve the goal.

Moving slowly, with his guidance, she felt the edge of the bed hit the back of her legs. Her dress was peeled from her body as he laid her on the soft bedcoverings. Without being told, she reached above her head and grasped the straps attached to the headboard. Hovering over her, he circled one turgid peak with his tongue.

"I could call you, my woman."

Maria gasped as he made the suggestion right before he clamped his teeth on her nipple, sucking it into his mouth. Her back bowed. The tug on the distended peak sent pleasurable jolts down to the tips of her toes. Releasing his victim, Ji-Yeong selected a new one.

"Or... I could call you, lover."

He continued his torture as he made his way down her body until he was resting, sniper style, between her spread legs. The sensation of him breathing on her exposed pussy had Maria writhing. Kissing her folds and pulling away with only a slight lick to the crease, Ji-Yeong looked up at her. His stare intense and purposeful.

"Or, I could simply call you, Mine. My Beauty. My Heart. My future."

Keeping his eyes on hers, he kissed the top of her mound with each proposal. "What do you have to say to that? Do I have your permission to say you are my everything?"

Maria's breath hitched. *He meant it.* It wasn't a game or simply sex. Ji-Yeong laid himself bare to her. How could she deny him?

"Yes. Yes, you have my permission. Do I have your permission to say you are *mine*?"

A broad smile took over Ji-Yeong's face. "I've been yours from the moment you looked at me, Beauty. The rest was just a formality."

Placing his hands on her inner thighs, he pressed them farther apart. "We'll talk logistics later. Right now, Honey wants to bless me with her cream. Isn't that right, Honey?"

Ji-Yeong's gaze was locked onto Maria's puffy nether lips. There was no mistake his last question was directed at her pulsing pussy. She had no complaints as her man drove her to her first orgasm of the night. Maria had no doubt there were more to come.

Epilogue

Eighteen months later

"Come on, Beauty. Time to put this stuff away."

Ji-Yeong walked into Maria's home office. His long fingers pushed the top of her laptop closed as he leaned over her desk to capture her lips. She sighed into the kiss, and he knew exactly why she didn't complain about his interruption. He was right. She was technically supposed to unplug thirty minutes ago. He'd given her a grace period.

Breaking the kiss with trailing pecks, Ji-Yeong lifted his head, but kept himself balanced on the desk with straight arms. One eyebrow rose on his forehead and he cocked his head to the side as he stared at her. Pushing back from the desk, his Beauty stood from the seat.

Standing to his full height, he extended his hand. Her fingers closed around his as she rounded the desk. Her outfit was business on top and ready for anything on the bottom. Not risqué, but the flirty skirt was definitely not something she'd normally wear into the office.

"I was almost done. You cut me off mid-email."

"As of twelve p.m., you're on vacation. Me and the boys have been waiting on you to come out of here so we can have lunch and get this party started."

"But what if—"

"They can wait until you get back. What's the point of you having all those Vice-Presidents if you can't take a week off to be with your family?"

Maria pouted, prompting Ji-Yeong to drop another kiss on her plump lips. He wrapped his arms around her. Their fronts were pressed together as he leaned down to speak directly into her ear.

"Don't give me that face, Beauty. We will skip lunch and I'll put you to work in a totally different way. These plump lips can keep busy wrapping around my cock while I fuck your mouth. Then, if you're a good girl, I'll eat your pussy and fuck you until you can't form thoughts coherent enough to respond to emails."

Maria's eyes rounded and her breath hitched. Ji-Yeong chuckled and nipped the crook of her neck. He loved knowing he could still do that to her—steal her breath with the promise of pleasure.

"Do you guys mind? Jared and I just want to have lunch. Not watch...whatever that is you two are doing over there." Ryu waved his hand in a circle in their direction.

Ji-Yeong ignored Ryu, and continued nuzzling Maria's neck. Her giggles encouraged him to continue to tease their sons, who groused about them being too old to not be able to keep their hands off each other. By now, they should be used to it.

Following their time together in Chicago, Ji-Yeong and Maria hadn't been apart for more than a week periodically. He still traveled, but his home base was with her in the home they purchased in Logan City. The new venture he'd started with other investors was best suited for being run in proximity to a major entertainment and travel hub like Atlanta.

Maria kept the home she lived in previously, turning it into a rental property. As it turned out, they had real estate in common as well. Except most of the properties she owned were in the area surrounding Atlanta and Logan City, while his was more international. Currently, they were at the villa in Bali. He'd converted a room in his private wing for her to have a home office.

Maria had begun actually using some of her personal time. Ji-Yeong learned she hadn't taken much time off after she returned from her hiatus when Oscar passed away three years before they met. She denied it, but he was certain it was guilt at having been absent for so long that kept her glued to her business responsibilities.

"Mama...please!" Jared took up where Ryu left off trying to put an end to Ji-Yeong's and Maria's show of affection.

Maria didn't immediately pull away. Instead, she reached around Ji-Yeong. She placed one hand on his ass, giving it a hefty squeeze.

"I do like how firm and squeezable you keep this bum-bum, Mr. Kang."

Mimicking her actions, Ji-Yeong did the same—only with both hands.

"And I like how these sweet cheeks feel in my hands, Mrs. Kang."

"Come on, guys. I think we get the point." Ryu groaned.

Ji-Yeong finally looked at their sons. Tilting his head, he stared at them.

"Do you really?"

Both young men nodded.

"Yes."

"So, tell us." Maria prompted. Ji-Yeong loved that shit. The way they were in sync with what the other was thinking.

"You are adults who love each other." Ryu began.

Jared supplied the rest. "You're allowed to be happy and express that."

Ji-Yeong nodded. Releasing Maria, he stepped back clasping her hand in his. Maria squeezed his fingers and tugged him toward the patio where the staff had lunch set up for them.

He couldn't be happier if he'd written the code to this relationship application himself. It was a little rocky in the beginning with their children. Ryu had never seen Ji-Yeong with anyone but his mom. The same was true for Jared. They each had to adjust to the new dynamic, but Ji-Yeong and Maria were united in their efforts to blend their families.

The key was actually getting the boys in the same place at the same time. When they realized their parents being together meant they now had a brother, they weren't quite as opposed to the change in their parents' status. They got along so well, it was almost impossible to tell they'd only known each other for a short time.

Their favorite thing to do was tell people they were brothers and watch the expressions on their faces as they tried to figure out how Jared, who was clearly African American, could possibly be blood related to Ryu, with his distinctly Korean features. Sometimes they'd put the person out of their misery. Often, they'd let them walk away with the look of confusion.

Pulling out Maria's chair, Ji-Yeong helped her sit before taking his seat next to her. Clasping her hand in his, he kissed her fingers. His eyes captured hers. The promise he silently made was received when she blushed and looked away.

Jared and Ryu's chatter picked up while they dug into their meal. Squeezing Maria's fingers, he let them go so they could both focus on their food. For a time, only their son's voices added to the normal island sounds surrounding them on the shaded patio.

Ji-Yeong took a moment to look at his family. He didn't think he'd ever have this again. But, he was grateful for the compulsion which drove him to Club Desire that fateful night. If he'd ignored it, he would've missed his opportunity to meet and capture the heart of his Beauty.

Being with Maria was something he'd ceased to hope for long before they met. He thought having playmates at the club, and the others like it he frequented around the world, had been enough. His Beauty changed everything for him the night they met.

They still played and kept their memberships current at the club. Whenever they were in the city, they liked to stop in to catch a performance. They'd even played on the dais a time or two. It turned out, his Beauty also had a bit of an exhibitionist in her to go with her voyeur kink.

Maria caught his gaze. Her brow lifted in silent question. Shaking his head, Ji-Yeong assured her everything was fine. Leaning closer, he kissed her cheek.

"I love you, Beauty."

"I love you too."

Her eyes searched his for a moment. Apparently finding what she was looking for, she pecked his lips. They both ignored their sons' renewed grumping about doing such things at the table.

Putting them out of their misery, Ji-Yeong picked up his fork to return to his meal. When they were done, Ryu and Jared wandered off to their section of the villa. Ji-Yeong vaguely noted them saying something about leaving before they were scarred for life, but he was too busy guiding his wife to their private suite.

As soon as the door closed behind them, he turned the lock and began stripping her out of the distracting skirt and deceptively demure top. Once she was bare and stretched out on the bed, he lay between her legs. His gaze was laser focused on her glistening folds.

"Do I have your permission to give Honey a kiss? She misses me and I haven't had my dessert yet."

Maria's hips tilted her fragrant pussy up toward his face and her fingers glided into his hair. Ji-Yeong didn't take her silent acceptance.

"I need your words, Beauty."

Maria's eyes blazed beneath her half-lowered lids.

"What kind of wife would I be if I denied my husband his pleasure of giving *me* pleasure? Yes. You have my permission."

Ji-Yeong groaned as he dove into her sweet haven. Her bliss was his as he drove her to her first orgasm. When he joined them together, he took his time stroking them to a joint release. It never failed to turn him on when she relinquished control allowing him to drive her desire to new heights—giving them both unparalleled pleasure.

The End

Acknowledgments

My sincere thanks to everyone who made this book possible. Thank you to the organizers of the Club Desire series for including me in this season. It has been a rewarding experience.

I have the best group of sister authors and readers behind me and it's amazing the ways they help me. To Niccoyan who writes with me each day, and is my first sounding board, thank you! To Brianna who reads my long messages where I share pieces of the story as I'm writing, you're awesome!

To my Beta readers who are always there with honest feedback, I sincerely appreciate you! Of course, none of this would be possible without the readers who continue to support me by purchasing and recommending my books to others. Y'all are amazing. Thank you so much!

Join our Facebook Group!

Want to be tapped in on all things Club Desire? Then join our Facebook Group and be first to know what's going on with the authors and future seasons.

Club Desire Reader's Group

Draft Pick Season I: Carver

EXCERPT

Prologue

Everyone's eyes were glued to the television as they listened to the commentators reviewing player stats. They waited anxiously for the actual draft to begin. Finally, the commissioner took the stage and Carver asked his girlfriend, Mary Beth to move to allow his mother to sit beside him. His dad stood behind him with his hands on Carver's shoulders.

Unlike most players being considered for the NFL draft, Carver had chosen to have a gathering to watch the televised broadcast rather than attend the event in person. His agent was noticeably unhappy about the decision, but he appeared to have resigned himself to the current arrangement. Sitting in an armchair near Carver's position, he intermittently called out instructions to the small camera crew.

Alyssa watched the scene play out between Carver and Mary Beth as her friend poked her bottom lip out, pouting prettily. A brief scowl flit across Carver's face. It only lasted a few seconds, but it was enough to get Mary Beth moving. Although, she didn't go far. She perched her narrow behind on the arm of the sofa, sliding in as closely as she could in order to stay in the frame of at least one of the cameras operated by the small crew.

Alyssa didn't consider herself a part of that inner circle. So, she sat off to the side sipping her fruity drink. Her thoughts regarding the interaction between Carver and Mary Beth would stay firmly locked inside her brain unless she was asked about it specifically.

Her gaze returned to the large, wall-mounted, flat screen TV just as the commissioner announced the first pick of the 2005 draft. As the analysts predicted, it was him, Tech's starting quarterback—Carver Wyatt Jamieson.

The room erupted in celebration. Camera flashes brightened the room as the video crew documented it all. No doubt it would be replayed on a loop during the endless cycle of sports shows that discussed the NFL draft for days to come. Carver smiled so big; she thought his face might split in two. His parents were alternately hugging him and each other.

Looking up from their embrace, his gaze swept the room as if he were looking for something. Feeling confident in her position on the periphery, she wondered what it could be, but didn't look around to track his stare. When his eyes landed on her, his face splitting smile brightened even more. His excitement was contagious. So, she returned the smile without hesitation. She was genuinely happy for him.

A tug on his arm broke their connection and Alyssa observed Mary Beth trying her best to insert herself into the middle of the circle his parents created. Tossing an arm around her shoulders, Carver pulled her into his side as he answered his cellphone. His mother fanned her hands and used shushing motions to quiet the room as Carver spoke with the owner of the team to which he'd just been drafted.

He was the number one draft pick of a team in the midst of rebuilding. If the sports experts were correct, the team was going to pay him a shit-ton of money to pull the franchise back to greatness. Alyssa was confident he'd do just that.

Her certainty wasn't misplaced. Carver was more than an impressive athlete. He was the total package. A true student of the game, he spent hours weekly pouring over old footage and scouting videos. In addition to his knowledge of the game, he was intelligent, considerate of his teammates, and kind to everyone he met while maintaining the ability to be ferocious when necessary.

Although she knew how he and Mary Beth met, she often wondered what kept them together. Mary Beth didn't quite match him in more than one of those areas. For all intents and purposes, her friend was in college to find a husband. Actual course study came in at a distant second. She'd never be accused of overtaxing her brain or spending too much time on her lessons, not leaving enough time for him.

She wondered at the tie binding them together, but Alyssa felt it wasn't her place to question their relationship. It wasn't like she wanted to date Mary Beth. Nor had Carver or anyone similar to him ever looked twice at her with more than a passing interest. Not that she lacked male attention. She just wasn't very interested in most of the guys who approached her.

As she watched the room, Carver's cousin slid into the seat next to her. She'd taken up residence at the high-top café style table slightly away from the festivities. Lord...She hoped he wasn't seriously there to hit on her. He was a nice-looking guy, but something about him didn't sit well with her.

"Hey there, beautiful. Why are you sitting over here all alone?"

Working to keep her internal eye roll from becoming an actual eye roll, Alyssa gestured around the room.

"These are the only available seats left." She was polite, but decidedly standoffish.

"Ah... I guess you're right. I hadn't noticed."

His chuckle at her response, came off as disingenuous since not only was her statement not funny, but she hadn't attempted to couch it as a joke. His smile appeared pasted on an otherwise placid looking face.

Studying the contents of her cup as if it held the secrets to deciphering the complex algorithm she had programmed for the final project in her Python class, she mentally wished him away. When she looked up from her cup, he was still there.

His stare tracked her movements as she placed the straw between her lips and drew deeply on the drink. *That's not creepy at all.* The thought crossed her mind accompanied by another internal eyeroll. The slurping noises of the empty cup were a welcome sound.

"Excuse me, I'm going to go get a refill." She scooted forward to step down from the tall chair.

"What are you drinking? I'll get it for you." He offered.

I think the fuck not. The words blared across Alyssa's mind, but instead of giving them voice, she politely declined.

"I appreciate the offer, but I can get it."

Thankfully, he got the hint and slinked away. Relieved that there wouldn't be a scene which turned into a thing to create awkwardness, she left the table and moved into the kitchen.

She was the designated driver, so she restricted herself to mocktails and sodas. Both Mary Beth and Carver had asked her to come tonight, although she couldn't figure out why. One-on-one interactions with Carver were few and far between, even though she never missed a game. Each Saturday, she was right beside her friend cheering him on—no matter what the weather.

At the start of the evening, Alyssa fully expected to drive back to the apartment she shared with Mary Beth alone. She figured her friend would stay with Carver either at the suite or at his apartment. Now, as Mary Beth entered the kitchen with her face pinched in displeasure, Alyssa wasn't so sure.

"Can you believe what just happened!?"

Mary Beth's face flushed and her cheeks pinkened under her peachy complexion. Her fists clenched at her sides as she strode to stand next to Alyssa at the kitchen island.

"What do you mean? Everyone knew Carver would go number one. Why is that a surprise? He's a great quarterback."

Alyssa refilled the ice in her cup before looking over the beverage selection trying to decide if she wanted to continue with the alcohol-free daiquiri mix.

"Not that. We all knew that." Flipping her long straw-colored hair over her shoulder she moved in closer to Alyssa. Glancing over her shoulder before she lowered her voice to continue. "Can you believe he asked me to move so his *mother* could sit beside him? That was supposed to be my spot! I've been his girlfriend for two years now."

She whisper-hissed when she said the word mother, and stopped just shy of stomping her foot with the last sentence. The whine in Mary Beth's voice annoyed her, but Alyssa kept her face neutral. She didn't personally have an issue with Carver wanting his mom beside him at such a crucial moment in his career. She actually expected it. *Why hadn't Mary Beth?*

"Mary Beth, why wouldn't he want his mother beside him?"

"Because! I'm going to be his wife. It should've been me holding his hand while they made the announcement. The same way it's been me for the past two years cheering for him and traveling to support him."

"Wait! Carver asked you to marry him?" Alyssa's eyes widened in excitement.

"Not yet, but I know he will." Mary Beth tipped her chin up as if her words were a foregone conclusion.

Alyssa's surprise melted into confusion. Her brow pinched as she regarded her friend. "How do you know that? Have you guys talked about it? You're still a month out from graduation."

Both Carver and Mary Beth were two years older than Alyssa. Because of the program she enrolled in, she wouldn't graduate until the following spring. When she did, she'd receive her bachelor's and master's degrees on the same day. It was a grueling program, but Alyssa felt it was worth it.

"Oh Alyssa... When you have someone that is into you the way Carver is into me, you'll understand. I'll be his wife. The rest is just minor details."

"Oh. Okay then. If you say so." Far be it for her to tell Mary Beth what could or couldn't happen in her own relationship.

"I do, which is why I'm pissed that I had to perch on the arm of the sofa like some hanger-on instead of being in my rightful place beside him."

"I think you're over-reacting."

"What?! Why?"

"That's his mother, Mary Beth." Alyssa struggled to keep her frustration from showing.

"And?"

Mary Beth's flip reply rubbed Alyssa the wrong way. So much so that she allowed the bridle, she usually kept on herself, to loosen when she responded.

"She's the woman who gave birth to him. The one who wiped his runny nose, patched his boo-boos and did any number of things to get him to this point in his life."

"I nursed him when he was sick and rubbed him down when he was sore, so what's your point?"

Not bothering to correct Mary Beth's statement regarding rubbing him down and nursing him through sickness, Alyssa took a calming breath. Her friend had selective memory. When Carver had soreness in his throwing arm and shoulder, it was Alyssa who rubbed him down—at Mary Beth's insistence. It was also the soup Alyssa made which Mary Beth fed Carver when he was sick.

Maybe merely asking Alyssa to physically do those things was what Mary Beth considered doing it herself. Like hiring staff. Alyssa didn't care for the image that evoked. Mentally, she shook herself and marveled at her friend's ability to hear what Alyssa said while missing the entire point.

"Mary Beth, you've done those things for roughly two years. His mother's been there for him for all twenty-two years of his life. She's the one who trekked all over the city then the country taking him first to practice, then games and God knows what else after that.

She's the one who sacrificed so he could have the opportunity to even be considered for the NFL draft. Her. Not you. Why would you expect to have more importance than her in his life right now?"

"Because! I'm going to be his wife! I should be more important. Aren't you always saying a husband should put his wife first?"

"Yes, but you aren't his wife. Going to be and being are not the same thing. Right now, you're his girlfriend. Girlfriend doesn't come before mother."

"I should have known you'd take his side." Mary Beth crossed her arms over her chest and angled her body away from Alyssa.

Sighing in irritation, Alyssa attempted to speak reasonably to her friend. "I'm not taking sides. I'm just pointing out some things you're over-looking."

"Well, it sounds like you're taking his side."

"Mary Beth, there are no sides here and if you want to know what I really think, I'll tell you."

"Don't stop now. This is apparently dump on Mary Beth night."

Shutting her lids against the wave of annoyance, Alyssa ignored the attempt to manipulate her into feeling guilty. Occasionally, Mary Beth could be self-absorbed. This wasn't the time or the place for her antics.

"I think you should pick your lip up off the floor and go back in that room and support your man. It's not about you right now. This is his moment. Acting this way, trying to make him choose between you and his mother, it won't end well for you. If you can't see that, I don't know what else to tell you."

Lifting her drink from the counter, Alyssa moved around Mary Beth and exited the kitchen. As she crossed the threshold, she almost ran smack into Carver's mother. Mumbling quick apologies, she stepped aside. Walking double-time, she went back to reclaim her seat at the high-top table.

Her cheeks heated with embarrassment as she considered the possibility that Carver's mother overheard them. If she heard even a portion of it, it was a bad look for Mary Beth. For her friend's sake, she hoped Mrs. Jamieson hadn't heard anything. However, Alyssa's gut told her that hope was wishful thinking.

Chapter One

IS THIS SOME KIND OF TEST?

Fifteen years later

"Hey, Mama. I can't talk long. I'm getting ready to go out." Alyssa rushed the words out as soon as she answered the insistently ringing phone.

"You're actually going out?" Surprise, along with disbelief laced her mother's voice.

Alyssa's eyes rolled in exasperation. So what if she didn't like going out all the time or taking the thirty minute drive into Vegas to live it up in the bright lights of Sin City. It didn't mean she was a complete hermit as her mother's question implied.

"Yes, Mama. I'm going out. I have a date with Torrence." Putting the call on speaker, she went back to the task of preparing for her date.

"Oh. Okay. Well, I won't hold you long." The line went silent as Alyssa waited for her mother to get to the point of her call.

She didn't miss the flat tone of her mother's speech when she heard *'going out'* included Torrence. It was no secret that Anna Ripley didn't think Torrence was worth Alyssa's time.

"What's up, Mama?" Alyssa attempted to keep her impatience from carrying over into her words, but her mama's version of not long usually meant at least twenty minutes. She didn't have twenty minutes to dawdle catching up on family gossip—which was usually why her mother called.

"Huh? Oh, sorry. Right. Your father and I were watching one of those sports reporting shows he likes earlier today and I saw your friend Carver. They said he has a new job as the Quarterback Coach with the Las Vegas Ravagers.

I thought to myself, I need to call Alyssa and see why she didn't tell me about it. So...Why didn't you tell me your friend from college was moving out there? You know how we worry about you being in Vegas all by yourself."

Alyssa's lids dropped over her eyes and her head tilted back on her shoulders. "Mama...First of all, Carver Jamieson and I aren't friends. We weren't friends in college. He dated my roommate Mary Beth and was friendly towards me. We weren't friends. Second, I don't follow football like that."

Even as she spoke the words, she knew her assertion of not following football was a blatant lie. She'd been known to rattle off stats better than both of her brothers and her father. Whether her mother would call her on it was the question.

"I had no idea he'd been hired by the Ravagers."

Another lie. She didn't live directly in Vegas, but she was close enough that her local news carried the story of the hotshot former pro-bowler who'd been hired by the Ravagers to spread his quarterback magic onto the struggling offense.

"And Third, I'm not out here by myself. Did you forget that Ulysses and Braxton live in Vegas?"

"Pssh! You know I don't count Ulysses and Braxton. You probably don't even hear from those two until it's close to a holiday and they want you to cook."

Alyssa couldn't dispute her statement since that's exactly when she heard from her two older cousins. Perpetual daters, neither was married and when the holidays rolled around, they either flew back to Georgia or called her to see what her plans were.

"Since when don't you follow football? I had as much trouble prying you away from the television for Sunday dinner as I did your father and the boys."

"I haven't been that into it in a while, Ma." *Why did she keep piling on the lies?* Alyssa had no answer for her sudden aversion to the truth.

"Mhmm. If you say so." It didn't sound as if her mother was buying it. "Back to Carver, I don't think we're remembering the same thing. He was always so nice to you. He talked like y'all were friends whenever we came up to see you at school."

"Mama, that was almost fifteen years ago. A lot can change in that time. Besides, I haven't seen him in a really long time. Why would you think we were friends?"

"Whenever your father brings him up, you always seem to know what's going on. I figured the two of you stayed in touch even after you and Mary Beth fell out. You know, I never liked that girl."

"Mama..."

Alyssa had no desire to go down memory lane about her former friend. Not simply because she didn't have the time, but her mother couldn't seem to stop once she got going on all the ways Mary Beth let Alyssa know they weren't really friends long before Alyssa cut her off.

"Don't Mama me."

"Mama, remember you said you weren't going to hold me long? I need to finish getting dressed." Attempting to thwart a possible lecture, Alyssa reminded her mother about the earlier promise.

"Mhmm. Fine. I'll just tell your daddy you didn't know about Carver, and that's why you didn't say anything." Once again, her mother spoke with the tone of disbelief.

"Okay, Mama. You have a good night. I'll call you in a few days." Relief washed over Alyssa when she realized she'd secured a slight victory. This time.

"Okay, baby. Love you."

"Love you too, Mama. Tell Daddy, I said hey and I love him."

Sighing at her good fortune, Alyssa finished with her date prep. She and Torrence were meeting at one of the casino restaurants at the edge of the Vegas strip. If she didn't get a move on, she'd be late.

She'd never tell her mother, but her level of affection toward Torrence was mediocre. While they had stimulating conversations, there was something holding her back from really seeing things with him moving beyond where they were.

It wasn't physical even though he wasn't the body type she normally went for. Since she found intelligence sexy, she didn't hold his slighter, lanky form against him. When they were together, they were a walking stereotype as one of her thighs was easily larger than both of his put together.

The thing about skinny men being attracted to plus sized women was in full effect. Putting the optics aside, he simply didn't make her stomach flip nor her nethers clench. Like ever. The few times they'd been together sexually had been pleasant but nothing to write home about.

Truth be told, she knew her days of entertaining Torrence were numbered. They'd refrained from saying what they had was an exclusive relationship, but they were approaching the six-month mark. It was time to step up or move on. Sadly, she didn't think it would hurt her feelings a bit if he were to break things off.

Apathy was never a good sign when considering a relationship with someone. Alyssa honestly wasn't sure if she was continuing to see him to prove something to herself or not. Most of her dating eligible life, she seemed to find herself enamored with someone who either didn't acknowledge her existence or only wanted to be friends with benefits. Both situations stung and didn't make the practice very appealing.

With Torrence, they seemed compatible in so many other ways. So what if he didn't make her heart race or her skin tingle. That type of passion fades over time. If she was to be with someone, it shouldn't be based solely on physical attraction.

Still, she knew the lack of passion wasn't an attractive prospect when considering tethering oneself to another person. Heaving a resigned sigh, she gathered her purse and keys before walking out of her townhouse.

Alyssa walked through the archway past the bistro tables sitting just outside the entrance to Wolfgang Puck's Lupo restaurant in the Mandalay Bay Casino. As far as casino restaurants went, she enjoyed eating here. The prices weren't so outrageous that she'd only delegate it for special occasions. Still, she wasn't inclined to shell out a hundred bucks on one meal very often. So, her visits weren't frequent.

After giving the hostess her name, she was led to a table just off the bar area where Torrence was already seated. Standing as she approached, he pressed a kiss to her cheek and pulled out her chair. While she didn't shrink away from his touch, she didn't lean in to it either.

"You look nice."

His eyes swept over her, examining her from her feet clad in peep toe pumps to the modest vee neck of her dress showing off the tops of her cleavage. She looked better than nice. The dress hugged her curves in all the best ways. Rather than correct him, she replied with a soft thank you as she took a seat in the chair he held out for her. Say what you will about Torrence, he played the gentleman thing to a T. *Most of the time.*

As she picked up the menu, he informed her that he'd already taken the liberty of ordering an appetizer.

"I didn't order your meal though. I know how you like do that yourself."

On the surface, his words appeared polite, but there was an edge to his tone as if he took offense to her having her own mind and ordering what she'd like to eat and not always yielding to what he wanted.

"Thank you." Alyssa replied as she opened the menu perusing it even though she was almost certain she would have the salmon. The question was really if she would pair it with the suggested wine or stick with water.

Their server approached the table just as she opted to forego the wine. Placing the Ciabatta bread appetizer at the center of the table, he pulled out the small folio flipping it open.

"Good evening. Have we decided what we're having tonight?"

"I have. Are you ready, Alyssa?"

Torrence hadn't even opened the menu before him. She figured he'd gotten there far ahead of their agreed upon time if he'd already made his selection. She hadn't arrived early, but she wasn't late either.

"I'm ready." Both men looked at her expectantly, so she lifted the menu once again. "I'll have the Scottish Salmon cooked medium please."

"Yes, ma'am. Would you care for a glass of wine with that? We have an excellent Cabernet Sauvignon that pairs quite well with the Salmon."

Torrence shifted in his seat and cleared his throat at the waiter's suggestion to add wine. He wasn't a fan of wine, but she didn't think his shifting was related to the drink itself. Thinking of the drive home and her potentially full stomach, Alyssa declined the offer with a smile.

"No, thank you. I'll stick with water for the time being."

"Yes, ma'am. And you, sir?"

"I'll have the ravioli. No wine for me either."

"Very good. I'll get this order in for you. Again, my name is Adrian. Please let me know if you need anything."

"Thank you, Adrian." Alyssa murmured as she passed him the menu.

After dating for the past few months, she'd noticed a pattern with Torrence. She really wished she hadn't but, it came with the territory of how her brain worked. Especially considering some life lessons she'd learned the hard way.

They went to nice places when they ate out. However, he tended to order the least expensive item on the menu. From everything he'd told her, he earned an excellent living at the accounting firm where he worked. He'd even mentioned that he was in consideration for partner. Which was admirable since he hadn't reached forty and had only been with the firm for five years.

She tried to shrug it off as him being frugal. Given his profession, that wasn't too far-fetched. Although she couldn't quite balance that against the times she invited him out and his tastes leaned toward more expensive menu items. His selections didn't bother her in regards to her ability to pay. Paying wasn't an issue.

The pattern was even more apparent tonight for some reason. Maybe it was because she was already on the verge of telling him to kick rocks. Considering the dating horror stories she heard from her girlfriends, her experiences with Torrence weren't anything to complain about. Still....

Their conversation over dinner was polite, but not overly stimulating. Movement at the bar caught Alyssa's attention, but she quickly returned her focus to what Torrence was saying.

"I can't find my wallet." His hands roamed his slender frame patting the pockets of his pants then reaching into the inner pocket of his jacket.

"Oh. Do you think you dropped it, or left it at home?" Concern wrinkled Alyssa's brow.

"No, I don't think I left it home, maybe I dropped it. But, I don't remember pulling it out since I've been here."

"Okay. Where's the last place you remember having it?"

Essentially done with her meal, Alyssa placed her knife and fork on her plate. Pushing it away, she gave him her full attention.

"I remember picking it up as I walked out of my apartment. I could have sworn I put it in my back pocket, but it's not there."

"Oh. Well maybe it fell out in your car. We can get the check and go look." Alyssa suggested.

"Get the check? Didn't I just say I couldn't find my wallet? How do you expect me to pay with no wallet? You know I don't trust those apps on the cellphone."

His voice was harsh and his dusky brown skin held a reddish under-tone that hadn't been present moments before. He was freaking out, but that was no excuse for him to take it out on her.

Before she could respond to his outburst he sat back in his seat. His body language in complete contrast to what it was only seconds before. *What in the entire hell?*

"What am I worried about? You've got me right? You shouldn't have any trouble forking over a hundred bucks on one meal. I do it every time I take you out. It won't hurt you to do it for a change."

Sitting there in his chair, his entire body relaxed. The smile on his face could only be described as smug. His demeanor set off warning bells in Alyssa's head. If she was reading the situation correctly, and she was positive she was, this was a test of some sort.

This was the part of dating she hated. The need some people had to test their potential mate, instead of coming straight out and communicating about what was bugging them, irked her. Heaven forbid they behave like adults and discuss the issues that bothered them.

Warmth crept up Alyssa's neck once the realization set in. They didn't even have a real relationship and he had the audacity to try to test her. To what end? To see if she was a Gold-digger? Refusing to play his game, she asked him.

"Torrence, did you really lose your wallet, or is this some type of test?"

"Why would you say something like that? Because I asked you to pay for a change?" Far from trying to keep their conversation between the two of them, he raised his voice above the conversational hum of the restaurant.

"First of all, there's no reason for you to get loud with me. It was a simple question. I told you in the beginning, I don't do games. I'm not about that life. Secondly, if you're nothing else, you're meticulous. There's no way you would be here without your wallet, unless you planned to put on an act to see if I'm only interested in you for your money."

"Well, are you?" He shot back immediately. Leaning forward, he put his elbows on the table.

"The fuck?" Alyssa's brow crinkled. Keeping her voice even, she decided to enlighten him on a few things.

"Torrence, I'm not sure what gave you the impression that I need your little check from being a drone at an accounting firm. I don't. Just because I don't brag about my ability to provide the way you do, doesn't mean I can't provide. It simply means I don't feel the need to broadcast it. I have nothing to prove to you or anyone else."

"I didn't say you had anything to prove. All I said was I pay all the time. I don't see why you can't pay this time."

"You asked me out. I didn't ask you. When I ask you, I pay. If you had a problem with that set up, you could've said something instead of pretending to lose your wallet to see what I would do. And in case you didn't notice, I *was* offering to pay. Then, I was going to help you look for the wallet that's probably in your damn pocket."

Pushing back from the table, Alyssa tossed the cloth napkin on her empty plate and swept her gaze over the room looking for their server. Catching Adrian's eye, she lifted a hand to call him over.

"What are you doing?" Torrence asked as if it weren't obvious. Ignoring him, she waited until Adrian stood next to the table.

"Yes, ma'am. Would you care for dessert or an after-dinner drink?"

"No. Thank you. Could you bring the check for the meal I ordered?"

If Adrian was shocked by her request, he covered it well as he immediately walked away.

"What the hell do you think you're doing?" Now, it seemed Torrence had learned volume control as he lowly growled his question.

"I'm giving you what you want. I'm paying for *my* meal, so you don't have to." Cool, dark amber, eyes regarded him as understanding filtered into his mind. He'd gambled. And lost.

"I didn't say you had to pay. Stop being a bitch."

Adrian chose that moment to reappear. Having already removed her wallet, Alyssa barely glanced at the receipt in the folio before placing three crisp twenty-dollar bills inside and passing it back.

"Keep the change."

"Thank you, ma'am." Adrian accepted payment and placed another folio in front of Torrence. "Whenever you're ready, sir." With that said, he quietly backed away.

Before he made it more than three steps, Alyssa was on her feet slinging her purse on her shoulder. Pushing her vacated chair to the table she glared at Torrence.

"I think it goes without saying, but I'll say it anyway. We're done."

"Done? You're acting like you were doing me some type of favor. You're lucky I even bothered."

Torrence was spoiling for a fight. Alyssa didn't care enough about him to give him any more of her energy. Shooting him a withering glance, she spun on her heel to leave and ran smack into a wall of man.

Chapter Two

GET OUT OF THE CAR ALYSSA

Carver's arms wrapped around Alyssa's soft body to steady her when she literally bounced off his chest. Assessing her strained visage, he reluctantly put some space between them.

"Are you okay? Is this guy bothering you?"

He wouldn't pretend he hadn't overheard the conversation between her and the guy she was intent on walking away from. He'd only caught a few words, but they were enough.

"I'm fine, Carver." If she was surprised to see him, she didn't let on. Pushing at his chest, she silently requested more room. As much as he wanted to deny her wish, he allowed it.

"Holy shit! You're Carver Jamieson."

No matter how many times it happened, he'd never understand why people felt the need to tell him who he was. He knew his own name. Years of experience allowed him to squash the outward appearance of annoyance.

Flicking his eyes to the obnoxious man behaving as if he wasn't being a complete ass to Alyssa just moments before, Carver blatantly disregarded his statement. Ducking his head, he peered into her face trying to capture her eyes.

"Are you sure you're okay?"

Rubbing her bare arms, she looked over her shoulder at her date. *Or whoever he was.* Tipping her chin up, she gifted Carver with a slight smile.

"Yeah. I'm good. Thank you."

"If you're good, why does your face look the way it did that time Professor Thigpen accused you of cheating?"

"It's nothing, Carver. Don't worry about it."

Her soft hand landed on his bare forearm sending a jolt to his system. He hadn't felt those hands on any part of his body in at least ten years.

"Don't lie to me, Bit." Slipping easily into the nickname he'd given her all those years ago, his gaze left her face to stare at her companion who now stood directly behind her.

"Yo, man. I've watched you play for years. Since your days at Tech. You're a living legend. Would you be cool with snapping a pic with me? My dad will never believe I met you not two days after they announced you'd joined the Ravagers. This is so cool."

The guy's lanky body practically vibrated with excitement. Had Carver not heard him being a such an asshole to Alyssa, he might have taken the pic and possibly even told him to call his dad on video chat. The problem is, he'd heard every venomous word the otherwise mild-mannered looking guy had said to her.

Heard it and didn't appreciate it. Moving Alyssa until she stood behind him, he ignored the pleading in her dark amber stare. He wasn't going to let it go. She should know that. He hadn't changed that much over the years.

"What's your name?" Carver asked, lulling the star-struck man into believing he would get exactly what he'd asked for. And he would. Just not the part where Carver would take a picture. The request his behavior and treatment of Alyssa made on his behalf.

"Torrence. Torrence Phillips."

Carver looked down at the hand extended to him, but didn't make a move to shake it. Instead, he folded his arms across his chest. While the move probably made him appear imposing, it was the only way he could keep himself from smacking the guy's hand away. Dude was either so star-struck that he couldn't pick up context clues, completely oblivious or such an asshole that he considered what Carver witnessed to be something easily brushed to the side.

"Torrence, I'm normally happy to accommodate a fan when I'm not in a rush."

"If you don't have time, I understand. I was just hoping to surprise my Pops."

"Oh, I have time. But I don't want to." The shocked expression on Torrence's face was priceless. Carver could tell he wanted to ask why, and before Torrence could jump to any conclusions, he told him.

"Why would I smile for the camera with a guy who's comfortable trying to embarrass a woman and refusing to pay for a date that *he* asked *her* on? Hard pass."

"What? That's why you're turning me down?" He held up a hand like he was being sworn in to testify. "I didn't say I wouldn't pay. She got all in her feelings and jumped to conclusions. Come on man. You of all people should know what it's like."

"Know what what's like?"

Carver inclined his head as if he actually wanted to know the answer and wasn't just letting Torrence talk himself into a hole.

"These women. They're always looking for a man to spend money, but they never think about reciprocating. I'm sure you've come across your share of Gold-diggers. You know what I mean."

"You know...You look like a smart man, but your elevator doesn't go all the way to the top floor does it?"

"I don't know what you mean."

Carver wondered if Torrence was aware he'd poked his lip out like a petulant child when he said that.

"Yes you do. You know exactly what I mean. Let me put it to you plain. I came over here because I heard you trying to shame this beautiful lady. Before I said a word to you, I checked on her. What kind of idiot would then think I'd take *his* side in that scenario?"

Understanding morphed Torrence's expression into anger coupled with embarrassment.

"Whatever man. I don't need a stupid picture with some washed up jock. If you're so concerned about a random fat black chick, you're welcome to feed her from now on. I warn you though. It ain't cheap. She likes food. Expensive food."

That's it. He'd had it. Lighting quick, Carver's arm shot out grabbing the slighter man by the front of the shirt. His fingers wrapped around the expensive tie and edges of his collar at the same time, lifting his thin body from the floor. A choked gasp pushed past Torrence's lips as he struggled to adjust to the sudden loss of air. Ineffective slaps rained against Carver's forearm as he tried to free himself.

"Who the fuck do you think you are to talk about her that way?" Carver's question was answered in another series of sputtering gasps because he'd literally cut off the other man's air supply. *If the only reason he used air was to insult Bit, he didn't need it.*

"Excuse me, Mr. Jamieson. I'm Mr. Hollister. Is there a problem?"

Carver cut his eyes to the white-haired man who appeared on his left side. "Nope. No problem."

Adjusting his tie against his crisp white shirt, the man spoke again. "Sir. I'm sure if you release the gentleman, we can discuss this and come to a positive resolution."

Returning his stare to the man flailing at the end of his wrist, Carver considered the words. The fingers of his other hand formed a fist as he contemplated knocking the douche out with a punch or letting oxygen deprivation do it for him.

He felt Alyssa's fingers wrap around his other arm, thereby taking the punching option off the table temporarily.

"Please, Carver." Her whispered plea reached his ears easily. "Please stop. People are looking." Pressing closer to him, she tugged at his arm. "They have their cameras out recording. Please stop."

Despite his desire to drive his fist into that asshole's disrespectful mouth, he listened to Bit and released his hold. The other man collapsed to the floor holding on to the edge of a chair to remain upright, desperately trying to refill the air in his lungs.

Under normal circumstances, Carver didn't get physical with men much smaller than him. It gave off bully vibes. These weren't normal circumstances and he'd be damned if he did nothing while the prick tossed insults at her.

"Thank you Mr. Jamieson. Now, if you could tell me what happened, I'm sure we can fix this."

Carver had almost forgotten the white-haired man was there. He must be the restaurant manager or somehow affiliated with the casino because the staff standing at his back deferred to him.

"He just choked me for no reason and you're trying to fix things with **him**?" From his position on the floor, Torrence's hoarse voice entered the conversation.

Alyssa's fingers tightened around Carver's forearm. Placing his right hand on top of both of hers, he squeezed her fingers in reassurance. He loved the feeling of her touching him and loathed the motivation behind it.

"Mr. Hollister, is it?"

"Yes, sir."

"I appreciate your attention to the matter, but I'm certain Mr. Phillips here understands my point and is going to make amends. Aren't you, Mr. Fredericks?"

Carver gave Torrence a pointed look as he watched him pick himself up from the floor and straighten his clothing.

"What?"

Carver inhaled deeply before releasing the breath. He understood the optics. As repugnant as he found the man, he was clear headed enough to understand how it could be interpreted with him as a well-known white man being in a confrontation with an African-American man.

"You were just telling me how you weren't going to allow Ms Ripley to pay for her own meal seeing as *you* asked *her* out. Right?"

The last word came from behind gritted teeth as his eyes shot daggers at the smaller man. "Right?"

"Uh... Yeah."

Maybe the man wasn't as dumb as Carver thought. Reaching into the inner pocket of his jacket, he pulled out his wallet. Picking up the black folio from the table, he slipped a credit card inside before handing it to the server standing nearby.

"Can you make sure to put the entire bill on this card and give the lady back her cash?"

"Don't bother." Alyssa spoke up. "I don't want it. I don't want another red cent from you."

Unsure of who to listen to, the server stood transfixed. Finally, Mr.

Hollister intervened instructing the young man to run the card and retrieve the cash. He returned in an astoundingly short amount of time.

One of the perks of being well-known. People in certain places tended to bend over backwards to be accommodating. Carver rarely took advantage of it, but he silently encouraged it in this instance.

"Here you are, ma'am. My apologies for the inconvenience." The young man held three twenty-dollar bills out to Alyssa. Folding her arms, she refused it.

"You keep it. Consider it a tip." Her face was set in stubborn refusal, Carver didn't press it.

"Thank you, ma'am!" The server made a hasty exit.

Tossing Alyssa's date one final look of disgust with a tinge of a threat to beat his ass, Carver slipped an arm around Alyssa's waist.

"Thank you for your assistance, Mr. Hollister. We'll get out of your hair now." If no one had seen him nearly strangle a man in the middle of a crowded restaurant, they wouldn't guess he'd been furious only moments prior.

Using his fingertips, Carver guided Alyssa from the restaurant by applying pressure to her lower back. Ignoring the blatant stares from around the restaurant, he escorted her through the faux outdoor seating, automatically leading them to the right.

Alyssa's steps faltered when they reached the corner at Citizen's Kitchen and Bar. His brow furrowed as he looked down at her questioning gaze.

"What's wrong, Bit?"

"Where are we going? I'm parked that way." Hitching a finger over her shoulder, she indicated the glass doors behind them which led to the outdoor parking area.

Should he tell her that his first instinct was to take her to his suite? He hadn't purchased a place yet, so he was renting one of the Presidential suites in the hotel. When he'd looked up from signing the check for the meal he'd eaten at the bar of the Lupo and seen her, his breath caught in his throat. It had been ten years, but when he saw her profile, it felt like just this morning that he'd awakened to an empty bed in Chicago.

"I was just thinking about getting you somewhere safe and away from prying eyes. So, I was heading to my suite. Besides, it's been a while, I figured we can catch up." *And talk about why you ghosted me.*

The last part he was smart enough not to say out loud, but the way she planted her feet said she heard it anyway.

"Oh, this is where you're staying?"

"Yeah. I haven't found a place, so I'm renting a spot here until I do. I have an appointment with a realtor to look at some places next week."

"Oh. Ok. Well, I appreciate you looking out for me, but I'm okay. I'm just going to head home now. It was good to see you though."

Carver's eyes said the words before he spoke them aloud. There was no way in hell he was allowing her to simply walk away. Even if he didn't want answers, he wouldn't simply let her go out into the night alone when she'd just had a verbal altercation with a disgruntled date.

"You know I'm not letting you go out there on your own, Bit. It's dark and you and your boyfriend just had a fight."

"He's not my boyfriend."

"Good to know." Using the hand he still had on her waist, he turned her until they were facing each other. "I'm still not comfortable with you driving off alone, but I'm willing to compromise."

"Carver, even if I were inclined to join you in your suite, I'm not up for walking all the way through a casino in these heels. These are for short distances and sitting." Lifting one foot, she rotated her ankle to display the four-inch heels which increased her height enough to put the top of her head close to his chin.

"Like I said, Bit. I'm willing to compromise. I'll walk you to your car. Then, you can drive us around to the hotel side. We can leave your vehicle with the valet and have a quick night cap. That way, I can feel sure you aren't out there alone just in case your little friend decides he wants revenge for being embarrassed."

Shaking her head and waving a dismissive hand, she refuted his assessment. "Torrence wouldn't do anything like that."

"How do you know? Did you ever think he'd do the things he did tonight?"

"No..." She dragged the word out, obviously not wanting to admit she may not know the guy as well as she thought.

Using the pressure of his fingertips, he rotated them both until they faced the doors leading to the parking lot. Without any further urging on his part, she started walking towards the doors. It didn't take them long to reach her SUV. Carver visually inspected the slate grey Lexus RX and gave a silent nod of approval at her choice.

Just as she started the vehicle, she gasped lightly. Had he not been so focused on her, he would have missed it.

"What is it?" Looking from her face, he followed her gaze out of the front window.

"It's nothing. I thought I saw something."

"Something like what?"

"Nothing. I'm sure it was just my imagination."

"Bit..." Placing a hand on her thigh, he gave it a squeeze. "If the thought was enough to cause you alarm. You need to tell me."

Biting her lower lip, Alyssa looked at Carver before returning her eyes to the well-lit parking lot. "I thought I saw Torrence's car drive by."

"Ok. So, he parked in the same lot and he's leaving. Good." As he said it, he knew if seeing Torrence leave was all there was to it, she probably wouldn't have acknowledged it.

"The car was going the wrong direction to leave the lot and it was moving really slow."

"What kind of car is it?"

"I don't know." At his expression, she explained more. "I don't pay much attention to cars to know the names of them."

"Ok...What does it look like?" Even though her lack of knowledge about the actual name of the vehicle didn't mesh with the detail-oriented person that she was, he tried to keep his voice neutral.

"It's red and low to the ground. I know it a sports car and it's supposedly really expensive."

"Ok. Do you still see it?" Scanning the area, he didn't see a vehicle matching the description she'd given.

"No." Pointing to the left, she continued. "I saw it between those two cars one aisle over. It could have just been my imagination overreacting to what you said earlier."

"Maybe." He said in a non-committal tone as he continued to study the cars and people in the parking area.

He remained quiet and observant as she maneuvered through the lot and traffic on the road to ferry them around to the hotel entrance. When she pulled into line behind the other cars, she turned to him and did exactly what he expected.

"Carver, I don't think I should come up. It's still relatively early in the evening, I should head home before it gets late."

Shaking his head, he pierced her with a knowing gaze. "That's not what we agreed to, Bit. Besides, if that guy really is riding around hoping to see you, I don't want you on the road alone."

"Carver, it's not your job to look out for me."

"Says who?" His brows dipped so low, his eyes became slits.

"Me. I'm an adult. I'll be fine. He doesn't know exactly where I live. We always met up. I never had him over."

"Bit, this isn't up for discussion." Pointing to the valet now standing at her door, he instructed, "Give the man your key and let's go upstairs."

Pressing the unlock button on his side of the vehicle, he nodded to the valet to open her door. Reaching over, he unbuckled her seat belt.

"Get out of the car, Alyssa."

His use of her given name had the desired effect. She passed the key fob to the valet and got out. When she'd fully exited the car, Carver unfolded his long frame from his seat, quickly meeting her at the front of the SUV.

She was correct. It was still relatively early by Vegas standards. Time would work in his favor, because they had things to discuss beyond how she ended up on a date with a douche who appeared to care very little about her. Even thinking about what the jerk said made Carver want to find the guy and pound his face in the way he desired in the restaurant.

About the Author

Darie McCoy is an independent author of contemporary, interracial, romantic suspense, and paranormal/shifter romance books. A reader first, she enjoys reading books across many genres although romance holds a special place in her heart. Her experience working in a STEM field offers her a unique perspective which she uses in each story she pens.

When she doesn't have her nose in a book or her fingers on the keyboard, Darie enjoys working in her vegetable garden. A serial hobbyist, she also enjoys knitting, sewing, baking and canning. One of her favorite treats to make is salted caramel popcorn. Amongst her friends, she's known to transport the sweet treat in large quantities to share whenever they get together.

Born and raised in the south, Darie stands by the staunchly held southern sentiments that the best tea is sweet tea and college football is life.

Also by Darie McCoy

Central Valley Pack Series

Chosen

Healed

Frost Family Series

For Real

Sano's Queen (A Novella)

Christmas Candy

Draft Pick Series

Draft Pick Season I: Carver

Draft Pick Season II: Andrei

Sin City MC Series (Collaboration with multiple authors)

Toad: Sin City MC Oakland

Other books/stories

Involuntary

Just Kiss Me (Part of Cupid's Kiss Anthology)

Power (Loving Hearts Loving Day Anthology)

www.ingramcontent.com/pod-product-compliance
Lightning Source LLC
Chambersburg PA
CBHW061251170626
46809CB00007B/2944